Canapes At
The Beach House Hotel

by

Judith Keim

BOOKS BY JUDITH KEIM

THE HARTWELL WOMEN SERIES:
The Talking Tree – 1
Sweet Talk – 2
Straight Talk – 3
Baby Talk – 4
The Hartwell Women – Boxed Set
THE BEACH HOUSE HOTEL SERIES:
Breakfast at The Beach House Hotel – 1
Lunch at The Beach House Hotel – 2
Dinner at The Beach House Hotel – 3
Christmas at The Beach House Hotel – 4
Margaritas at The Beach House Hotel – 5
Dessert at The Beach House Hotel – 6
Coffee at The Beach House Hotel – 7
High Tea at The Beach House Hotel – 8
Nightcaps at The Beach House Hotel – 9
Bubbles at The Beach House Hotel – 10
Canapes at The Beach House Hotel – 11
Sea Breezes at The Beach House Hotel – (2026)
THE FAT FRIDAYS GROUP:
Fat Fridays – 1
Sassy Saturdays – 2
Secret Sundays – 3
THE SALTY KEY INN SERIES:
Finding Me – 1
Finding My Way – 2
Finding Love – 3
Finding Family – 4
The Salty Key Inn Series – Boxed Set

.

LILAC LAKE BOOKS

Love's Cure

Love's Home Run

Love's Bloom

Love's Harvest

Love's Match – (2026)

OTHER BOOKS:

The ABCs of Living With a Dachshund

Trouble At The Winston Hotel... A Mouse Mystery

Holiday Hopes

The Winning Tickets

For more information: **www.judithkeim.com**

PRAISE FOR JUDITH KEIM'S NOVELS

THE BEACH HOUSE HOTEL SERIES – Books 1 – 10:

"Love the characters in this series. This series was my first introduction to Judith Keim. She is now one of my favorites. Looking forward to reading more of her books."

BREAKFAST AT THE BEACH HOUSE HOTEL – *"An easy, delightful read that offers romance, family relationships, and strong women learning to be stronger. Real life situations filter through the pages. Enjoy!"*

LUNCH AT THE BEACH HOUSE HOTEL – *"This series is such a joy to read. You feel you are actually living with them. Can't wait to read the latest one."*

DINNER AT THE BEACH HOUSE HOTEL – *"A Terrific Read! As usual, Judith Keim did it again. Enjoyed immensely. Continue writing such pleasantly reading books for all of us readers."*

CHRISTMAS AT THE BEACH HOUSE HOTEL – *"Not Just Another Christmas Novel. This is book number four in the series and my introduction to Judith Keim's writing. I wasn't disappointed. The characters are dimensional and engaging. The plot is well crafted and advances at a pleasing pace.*

MARGARITAS AT THE BEACH HOUSE HOTEL – *"Overall, Margaritas at the Beach House Hotel is another wonderful addition to the series. Judith Keim takes the reader on a journey told through the voices of these amazing characters we have all come to love through the years!*

DESSERT AT THE BEACH HOUSE HOTEL – *"It is a heartwarming and beautiful women's fiction as only Judith Keim can do with her wonderful characters, amazing location. and family and friends whose daily lives circle around Ann and Rhonda and The Beach House Hotel.*

COFFEE AT THE BEACH HOUSE HOTEL – *"Great story*

and characters! A hard to put down book. Lots of things happening, including a kidnapping of a young boy. The Beach House Hotel is a wonderful hotel run by two women who are best friends. Highly recommend this book.

HIGH TEA AT THE BEACH HOUSE HOTEL – "What a lovely story! The Beach House Hotel series is a always a great read. Each book in the series brings a new aspect to the saga of Ann and Rhonda."

THE HARTWELL WOMEN SERIES – Books 1 – 4:

"This was an EXCELLENT series. When I discovered Judith Keim, I read all of her books back to back. I thoroughly enjoyed the women Keim has written about. They are believable and you want to just jump into their lives and be their friends! I can't wait for any upcoming books!"

"I fell into Judith Keim's Hartwell Women series and have read & enjoyed all of her books in every series. Each centers around a strong & interesting woman character and their family interaction. Good reads that leave you wanting more."

THE FAT FRIDAYS GROUP – Books 1 – 3:

"Excellent story line for each character, and an insightful representation of situations which deal with some of the contemporary issues women are faced with today."

THE SALTY KEY INN SERIES – Books 1 – 4:

FINDING ME – "The characters are endearing with the same struggles we all encounter. The setting makes me feel like I am a guest at The Salty Key Inn...relaxed, happy & light-hearted! The men are yummy and the women strong. You can't get better than that! Happy Reading!"

FINDING MY WAY- "Loved the family dynamics as well as uncertain emotions of dating and falling in love. Appreciated the morals and strength of parenting throughout. Just couldn't put this book down."

FINDING LOVE – "Judith Keim always puts substance into her books. This book was no different, I learned about PTSD, accepting oneself, there are always going to be problems but stick it out and make it work.

FINDING FAMILY – "Completing this series is like eating the last chip. Love Judith's writing and her female characters are always smart, strong, vulnerable to life and love experiences."

"This was a refreshing book. Bringing the heart and soul of the family to us."

THE CHANDLER HILL INN SERIES – Books 1 – 3:

GOING HOME – "I was completely immersed in this book, with the beautiful descriptive writing, and the author's way of bringing her characters to life. I felt like I was right inside her story."

COMING HOME – "Coming Home was such a wonderful story. The author has such a gift for getting the reader right to the heart of things."

HOME AT LAST – "In this wonderful conclusion, to a heartfelt and emotional trilogy set in Oregon's stunning wine country, Judith Keim has tied up the Chandler Hill series with the perfect bow."

SEASHELL COTTAGE BOOKS:

A CHRISTMAS STAR – "Love, laughter, sadness, great food, and hope for the future, all in one book. It doesn't get any better than this stunning read."

CHANGE OF HEART – "CHANGE OF HEART is the summer read we've all been waiting for. Judith Keim is a master at creating fascinating characters that are simply irresistible. Her stories leave you with a big smile on your face and a heart bursting with love."

~Kellie Coates Gilbert, author of the popular Sun Valley Series

A SUMMER OF SURPRISES – "Ms. Keim uses this book as an amazing platform to show that with hard emotional work, belief in yourself, and love, the scars of abuse can be conquered. It in no way preaches, it's a lovely story with a happy ending."

A ROAD TRIP TO REMEMBER – "The characters are so real that they jump off the page. Such a fun, HAPPY book at the perfect time. It will lift your spirits and even remind you of your own grandmother. Spirited and hopeful Aggie gets a second chance at love and she takes the steering wheel and drives straight for it."

THE BEACH BABES – "Another winner at the pen of Judith Keim. I love the characters and the book just flows. It feels as though you are at the beach with them and are a part of you.

THE DESERT SAGE INN SERIES – Books 1 – 4:

THE DESERT FLOWERS – ROSE – "The Desert Flowers - Rose, "In this first of a series, we see each woman come into her own and view new beginnings even as they must take this tearful journey as they slowly lose a dear friend.

THE DESERT FLOWERS – LILY – "The second book in the Desert Flowers series is just as wonderful as the first. Judith Keim is a brilliant storyteller. Her characters are truly lovely and people that you want to be friends with as soon as you start reading. Judith Keim is not afraid to weave real-life conflict and loss into her stories.

THE DESERT FLOWERS – WILLOW – "The feelings of love, joy, happiness, friendship, family, and the pain of loss are deeply felt by Willow Sanchez and her two cohorts Rose and Lily. The Desert Flowers met because of their deep feelings for Alec Thurston, a man who touched their lives in different ways."

MISTLETOE AND HOLLY – "As always, the author never ceases to amaze me. She's able to take characters and bring them to life in such a way that you think you're actually among family. It's a great holiday read. You won't be disappointed."

THE SANDERLING COVE INN SERIES – Books 1 – 3:

WAVES OF HOPE – "Such a wonderful story about several families in a beautiful location in Florida. A grandmother requests her three granddaughters to help her by running the family's inn for the summer. Other grandmothers in the area played a part in this plan to find happiness for their grandsons and granddaughters."

SANDY WISHES – "Three cousins needing a change and a few of the neighborhood boys from when they were young are back visiting their grandmothers. It is an adventure, a summer of discoveries, and embracing the person they are becoming."

SALTY KISSES – "I love this story, as well as the entire series because it's about family, friendship, and love. The meddling grandmothers have only the best intentions and want to see their grandchildren find love and happiness. What grandparent wouldn't want that?"

THE LILAC LAKE INN SERIES – Books 1 – 3:

LOVE BY DESIGN –"Genie Wittner is planning on selling her beloved Lilac Inn B&B, and keeping a cottage for her three granddaughters, Whitney, the movie star, Dani an architect, and Taylor a writer. A little mystery, a possible ghost, and romance all make this a great read and the start of a new series."

LOVE BETWEEN THE LINES – "Taylor is one of 3 sisters who have inherited a cottage in Lilac Lake from their grandmother. She is an accomplished author who is having *some issues getting inspired for her next book. Things only get worse when she receives an email from her new editor with a harsh critique of her last book. She's still fuming when Cooper shows up in town, determined to work together on getting the book ready."*

LOVE UNDER THE STARS – *"Love Under the Stars is the third book in The Lilac Lake Inn Series by author Judith Keim. Judith beautifully weaves together the final story in this amazing series about the Gilford sisters and their grandmother, GG."*

THE LILAC LAKE BOOKS

LOVE'S CURE – *Welcome back to Lilac Lake with a new spin-off series from author Judith Keim. For fans of the author, you will be reunited with previous characters, as well as being introduced to new ones. Even though this book can be read as a stand-alone, I highly recommend reading the Lilac Lake Inn series to get introduced to all of these amazing characters.*

Canapes At
The Beach House Hotel

The Beach House Hotel Series
Book 11

by

Judith Keim

Wild Quail Publishing

COPYRIGHT

Canapes at The Beach House Hotel is a work of fiction. Names, characters, places, public or private institutions, corporations, towns, and incidents are the product of the author's imagination or are used fictitiously. Any resemblance to actual events, locales, or persons, living or dead, is coincidental.

No part of *Canapes at The Beach House Hotel* may be reproduced or transmitted in any form or by any electronic or mechanical means, including information storage and retrieval systems, without permission in writing from the author, except by a reviewer who may quote brief passages in a review. This book may not be resold or uploaded for distribution to others. For permissions, contact the author directly via electronic mail:

wildquail.pub@gmail.com
www.judithkeim.com

Wild Quail Publishing
PO Box 171332
Boise, ID 83717-1332

DEDICATION

To all my readers who enjoy food as much as my family does!

CHAPTER ONE

EARLY ONE SUNNY SEPTEMBER AFTERNOON, MY BUSINESS partner and best friend, Rhonda Grayson, and I sat in our office at The Beach House Hotel in the town of Sabal on the Gulf Coast of Florida.

We'd just received a call from Vice-President Amelia Swanson giving us a heads-up that the Italian Ambassador to The United Nations in New York City had called her asking for a recommendation of a hotel in Sabal, Florida.

"I told him there's no better place than The Beach House Hotel, "Amelia said. "If he calls for a reservation, please pamper him, maybe put him in the Presidential Suite. Can you do that for me? It would be most helpful."

"Of course," I said, holding back a sigh. Doing favors for Amelia had always gotten Rhonda and me in trouble. I didn't think this would be any different, but what could we say? Our hotel had hosted many interesting, sometimes famous people. Some were easy. Some were not.

"Thank you both very much," said Amelia. "Hope to see you when I'm next in Sabal."

The call ended, and I turned to Rhonda. "Let's go for a walk on the beach. I need some fresh air. I have a feeling this will involve a lot of extra work for us."

We eagerly left the office.

As we walked through the luxurious lobby of the hotel, Rhonda nudged me. "Hey, Annie, see that young couple sitting at the bar? I greeted them the other day, and the man said he liked to taste-test our canapés. I know we own an upscale hotel, but that sounded like a fancy name for appetizers. What's up with that?"

"Canapés has an elegant ring to it, don't you think?" I said, throwing my arm around her. Rhonda and I were as different as two partners could be. She grew up in a tough, Italian immigrant neighborhood in New Jersey, and I was raised by a cold, proper grandmother in Boston who would've fainted if I'd ever dropped an F-bomb, one of Rhonda's favorite words.

"Sounds like B.S. to me," grumped Rhonda.

"Oh, but I love the idea of offering upscale food to our guests," I said. "Let's go talk to that couple and see what they're up to."

We walked into the bar and over to the two who seemed to be in their early thirties—the same age as our two grown daughters. He was swirling his white wine in a glass and sniffing its bouquet, while the woman sat beside him and looked out through the windows, which offered a dynamic view of the adjacent beach.

The woman, a small, pretty one with strawberry-blond hair and green eyes, touched his arm as we approached, and I heard her say, "Chet, I think the owners want to speak to us."

The man beside her swiveled on the barstool to face us. "Ann Sanders and Rhonda Grayson, I believe," he said, getting to his feet to greet us. "Nice to meet you. I'm Chet Waring, and this is my friend, Harper Lewis."

Of above average height and with broad shoulders, Chet stared at us with startling topaz eyes. His dark hair flopped an errant curl onto his forehead.

"Rhonda says she's seen you here before," I said.

"That's true, we met the other day," said Chet. "I love checking out the appetizers and canapés. You can tell a lot about a restaurant from its offerings. I've heard of Jean-Luc Rodin, of course, and wanted to see for myself the operation he runs and how he manages to maintain his outstanding reputation.

"The real way to sample his food is by eating dinner here," said Rhonda. "That's where he shines."

"We're both looking for jobs and wanted to see if The Beach House Hotel would be a workable fit for us," Harper said. "That's why we're checking it out, among other places."

Rhonda and I exchanged surprised glances. Most people wouldn't bother with comparisons. We treated our employees very well.

"What work are you looking for?" I asked.

"Well, I'm a chef with a story, and Harper is very versatile in any restaurant setting," said Chet, smiling at his companion.

"We can't work for just anyone," said Harper. "There must be a great deal of trust between the employer and employees."

"Why don't you two come to our office to talk further? Maybe tomorrow afternoon?" I said, glancing around to make sure no one else could hear. We were very private about certain discussions in public in our hotel, all part of the commitment to protect the privacy of our guests.

"I want to talk more about those canapés you keep referring to," said Rhonda.

Chet looked at Harper. "Should we do it?"

"Oh, yes," she replied and turned to us with an apologetic look. "We don't mean to hesitate. It's just that we've had a bad experience."

"I'll explain it to you when we meet," Chet said.

"Okay, see you tomorrow," I said, curious about them.

Rhonda and I left them and headed to the beach where we did some of our best thinking.

At the beach's edge, I flipped off my sandals and buried my toes in the warm sand. Sighing with pleasure, I inhaled the salty air and stared up at the blue sky where marshmallow puffs of clouds glided lazily across it. I tiptoed across the sand and sank my feet into the frothy edge of the cooler water, holding my sandals high above it.

The waves rolled in to shore one after the other in a rhythm as old as time. It comforted me to hear the kiss of them meeting the sand and pulling away for another chance to do it all over again.

Rhonda lifted the bottom of her caftan into her arms and joined me at the water's edge.

"Feels good, huh?" she said, smiling at me.

"Heavenly." I looked up as someone called my name. "Uh-oh. Guess who's headed our way."

"It'd better not be ... damn!" sputtered Rhonda.

"Hello, ladies," said Brock Goodwin, the president of the Neighborhood Association. Seeing him here this time of day could only mean trouble.

"What do you want?" said Rhonda. Neither of us could stand the man who was always trying to hurt the business we ran so proudly.

"I thought you should know about my latest venture," Brock said smoothly. He was a good-looking older man with silver hair, a trim physique, and enough manufactured charm to be sought after by single women in the area looking for a date to accompany them to a social event.

"What are you up to now?" growled Rhonda.

"I'm a part-owner of a fantastic new Italian restaurant just up the beach. It's for people looking for a change from a hotel restaurant, something in a creative space just for them," Brock sniffed. "We're offering fabulous food, location, and space for those wanting a superior dining experience."

"What is it called?" I asked, unable to resist wanting more details.

"Osteria Arno," said Brock.

"Who's your chef?" I asked.

"Jonny Arno," said Brock. "He's the best, you know."

"Depends," Rhonda said, and I silently pleaded with her not to say more.

She glanced at me and whatever she was about to say faded in her mouth.

Brock gave us a smug look. "I think this investment of mine is going to pay off in a big way. Even Jean-Luc will want to come to Osteria Arno. Jonny can show him a thing or two. You girls need to have some decent competition. Then we'll see what kind of businesswomen you really are."

"Thank you for your concern," I said through clenched teeth. "But we don't need to prove anything to anyone. The success of our hotel speaks for us."

"Why don't you run along, Brock. We have important things to discuss. Business that has nothing to do with you," said Rhonda,

"You'll see. The day will come when you're asking favors of me. Jonny says I can be a big help to him." Brock gave us a wave and trotted away.

Rhonda and I stared at him, sighing in unison.

"How can anyone like that survive?" asked Rhonda. "He's pissed off enough people to be in danger of someone finally giving in to the temptation of wringing his fucking neck."

"As long as that someone isn't you," I said. "We have a hotel to run. Together."

"Seriously, Annie, what are we going to do about competition like Osteria Arno? If Brock's involved, it'll mean nothing but trouble for us."

I swung my arm across Rhonda's shoulder. "That, dear partner, is what we are about to find out."

After Chet and Harper arrived for their meeting the next afternoon, I was as curious as Rhonda as we indicated for them to sit at the small conference table with us.

"Now, do you want to talk about your situation? We'd like to hear it," I said.

"All of it," added Rhonda.

"I guess I'll begin with how the trouble started," said Chet.

Harper nodded her agreement.

"But first, some very important history for you," said Chet. "I was raised in upstate New York, and when I was six years old, my father was killed in Afghanistan, leaving my mother and me alone. Our neighbor, Rosalie Mancini, took care of me while my mother was at work. Two years later, my mother married a man who, to put it bluntly, hated me. So, at eight, I spent a lot of time with Rosalie even after my mother and stepfather moved to a different house in the same neighborhood."

As Chet stopped to take a drink from the glass of water I'd placed before him, Harper said quietly. "All of it is important."

"While we were together, Rosalie taught me to cook," continued Chet. "It was a creative outlet and she and I became very close. And when she realized how much my stepfather belittled me for liking to cook, she spoke to my mother about it. And though things got better, my stepfather thought I should've been playing football, not busy in a kitchen like a girl. Privately, he called me every name he could think of. None of them nice."

I could see Rhonda's fingers begin to curl into a fist and knew how upset she was. Rhonda herself had used cooking to get through tough times growing up in her neighborhood.

"So, that's where and how you learned to cook," I said, prompting him to continue.

"Yes, but our cooking wasn't about following recipes. It was more than that. It was about smelling and tasting food, trying new combinations, putting creativity into food that gave people pleasure."

"My grandmother taught me to cook that way, too. I've been forever grateful to her. Like your Rosalie, she saved my life," said Rhonda. "Go on."

"I graduated from the Culinary Institute of America in Hyde Park, New York, ten years ago and chose to move to warm weather after Rosalie died. Rosalie had always wanted to be able to go to Florida, but never did. So, I thought that would be a good place for me to start fresh."

"How did the two of you meet?" I asked Harper.

"I was getting my college degree in psychology from the University of Miami and had to work my way through school. I started waitressing, then tending bar, where I could make a lot more money," said Harper. "My last job was at Chez Michel. Do you know it?"

"I do," said Rhonda. "The chef, Jonny Arno, recently put out a new cookbook. An Italian one. I bought it. It's fabulous, with recipes my grandmother would love, with an international flair."

"Exactly," said Chet, his cheeks flushing with emotion. "The problem is that a lot of those recipes were stolen from me. When I confronted Jonny about it, he fired me, and told me he'd see to it I'd never work in Miami again or anywhere else."

"Are you sure they were your recipes? Plagiarizing is illegal," I said. "How could you be certain?"

Chet's lips thinned. "I'm sure. Some of the recipes he stole were from a notebook I'd mistakenly left in my locker one night. Rosalie's secret ingredients were in some of them. Enough to be of concern. And when I looked at the recipes he'd put in his book, the instructions matched exactly."

I shook my head. "That's not fair, but it's a difficult thing to prove."

"Some recipes require the same ingredients from any source," said Rhonda. "Even the extras you talk about are hard to declare as your own."

"But he made up a story about a friend named Rosalie. That's another thing that can't be called just a coincidence," said Chet. "That's what hurts the most. Rosalie would never have allowed a man like him to use her recipes. For all the PR Jonny Arno gets, the people who work for him hate him, and for a reason. I'm not talking about the usual temperamental chef behavior but an evil man who's willing to destroy someone else with cruelty."

Harper put a hand on Chet's arm in sympathy. "Chet's right. Jonny Arno is not a great person. He persisted in trying to seduce me even after I made it clear I was not going to bed with him." She let out a snort. "When I threatened to say something, he was furious and told me I was too ugly for him anyway."

"Why hasn't all this been reported?" I asked and then said, "Forget that. I understand why no one would want to be tormented even more by him. He sounds like a real monster."

"That's a perfect name for him," said Chet. "I think he found out another chef was interested in bringing me on board. But after my trouble with Jonny, no one would even respond to my calls. That's why I'm here, hoping that I can find work on the Gulf coast of Florida. Someplace safe."

"Are you two aware that Jonny Arno is opening a restaurant not far from here?" I asked, and saw their faces fall. "Rhonda and I would like to think about how we might be able to help you. The hotel business is a tough one, but there's no need for cruelty and deception."

"Absolutely," said Rhonda. "Let us do a little investigation, and then we'll be in touch with you to set up another meeting."

After we showed them out of the office, Rhonda turned to me with a frown. "Do we really want to get involved with Chet and Harper? This news of Osteria Arno changes things. He might be vindictive toward us."

"Knowing Brock is somehow involved in the restaurant is troublesome," I admitted. "He'll make a bad situation worse, and from what I've seen of them, Chet and Harper seem like decent kids. Let's do some research of our own before we meet with them."

"Okay," said Rhonda. "I don't think these kids can handle a comeback on their own. I know what kind of people sometimes get involved with supplying restaurants. My father had to deal with them when he opened his butcher shop in Jersey."

"Do you think it's dangerous for us to try and help Chet and Harper? Maybe even hire them?" I asked, appalled by the idea of dealing with people who could really hurt us.

"I think we need to be careful. That's all," said Rhonda.

CHAPTER TWO

RHONDA AND I DECIDED TO GO TALK TO JEAN-LUC.

When he saw us approaching, he raised his eyebrows. "What brings you to my kitchen at such a busy time?"

The question held a bit of reproach.

"Sorry to interrupt you," I quickly said. "Do you have a moment to talk to us?"

He looked up at the wall clock. "Okay."

He led us to his office and stood waiting for us to speak. I knew he wasn't necessarily being rude; he was just aware of his time before creating another successful dining experience at The Beach House Hotel.

"What do you know about Jonny Arno?" Rhonda asked.

"He's opening a restaurant up the beach from us," I added.

Jean-Luc frowned and shook his head. "*Il est un bâtard. Difficile.*"

"In English?" Rhonda said.

"He's known as a real bastard, very difficult. His ego outweighs his body, if that's possible. He's lazy and out-of-shape from the rich food he has others make for him."

"Wow!" Rhonda said. "You really don't like him."

"No," Jean-Luc said. "I don't trust him at all. And as for the restaurant he claims he's opening, it will be left to others to do all the work, though he'll take the credit for it."

"Let us tell you about a young man we just met who's looking for a job in the kitchen. A C.I.A graduate with ten-plus years of experience, he's been blackballed in Miami for accusing Chef Arno of stealing his personal recipes. The chef made sure he'd never work in Miami, which is why he's looking for work on the Gulf Coast ," I explained.

"We're going to talk to him and his friend, a bartender, to try and help them," said Rhonda. "Would you be open to having him work in your kitchen?"

Jean-Luc shrugged. "If he's qualified and willing to work hard, I'll see."

"That's all we're asking. We understand the decision is yours, not ours," I said to Jean-Luc. We'd do nothing to abuse our respect and gratitude for him.

"I'm going to look into this new restaurant coming to the area. What else do you know about it?" Jean-Luc asked.

"The name of it is going to be Osteria Arno," said Rhonda, "and that bastard, Brock Goodwin, is apparently an investor of sorts."

"Already it doesn't sound good," said Jean-Luc. "Let me see what else I can find out about it, and I'll get back to you. After talking with the young chef tomorrow, if you're satisfied that he's an excellent candidate, I'll do my own evaluation."

"Thank you, Jean-Luc," I said, as he turned away.

"That was an interesting conversation," said Rhonda. "I'm very curious to discover more about the young canapé chef."

"And his charming girlfriend. I'm thinking she'd be someone to hire for the cocktail hour shift, so she can help to attract a younger crowd the girls want us to focus on."

"Why don't we ask Liz and Angela to interview her? That will give them a chance to participate in the hotel and will help us decide if we want to go ahead with a program aimed at young married and dating couples."

"Smart idea," I said. "I know how limited their time is as they tend to their growing families. But we need to keep our daughters' interest up in helping us with the hotel so that they'll be ready to take over for us someday."

"With seven young children between the two of them, it's difficult for them to work here," Rhonda said. "But, like you, I don't want them to lose their enthusiasm for running the hotel in the future."

"I'm going to call Liz now to see when she and Angie could come to the hotel to meet with Harper," I said, pleased for the opportunity to speak to my daughter. With almost five-year-old triplets and an eighteen-month-old baby boy, Liz didn't have the time for much else. I punched in Liz's number.

"Hi, Gammy," said a voice I recognized as Olivia's. My name had changed a few times, but had ended up as Gammy when Noah declared it was the best one. His sisters, Olivia and Emma, went along with it.

"Hi, Sweetheart. Is Mommy there?"

"Yes, hold on please," said Olivia, acting as her mother's self-important helper.

Chuckling, I waited for Liz to get to the phone.

"Hi, Mom. What's up?" Liz asked.

"I want to run an idea by you," I said. "But first, I need to compliment Olivia on her phone manners. She did very well."

"We've worked hard on that. I'll be happy to tell her she did a great job. How are you?"

"Busy as ever at the hotel. Rhonda and I thought you and Angie might like to interview someone for a bartender position at the hotel's Lobby Bar. She's young but apparently talented at her job. We're doing a background check now. We thought she'd be perfect for the campaign you and Angie are putting together to bring in a younger crowd."

"What's the timing?" Liz asked. "I can juggle things around a bit."

"Rhonda and I are meeting with her and her friend, a chef, tomorrow afternoon. Perhaps sometime later or the day after that, if we're confident they'd be a match for us."

"Yes, I think I can do that. My babysitter will be here then. So, what's their story? You mentioned a bartender and a chef."

I filled Liz in on the details.

When her toddler, Gabe, started crying, Liz said, "Let me know what time Angie has free, and I'll work something out. Thanks, Mom. I appreciate having the opportunity to do something creative for the hotel."

"I know, darling," I said, hearing the weariness in Liz's voice. "Let's do lunch soon."

We ended the call, and I sat back in my chair to listen as Rhonda completed her call with Angela.

"Angie said she'll work out a time with Liz. She loved the idea of hiring a young person to handle early evening bar service." Rhonda sighed. "She also told me that Sally Kate has been diagnosed with dyslexia. She's having trouble reading."

"I imagine it's both a worry and a help that she's been classified as dyslexic," I said.

"Sally is a sweet child who has been suffering under the impression that she's stupid," sighed Rhonda. "Angela is determined to see that Sally Kate understands why she's been having difficulties, that it has nothing to do with ability."

"It's so important," I said. "Kids today have a hard enough time socially without any additional issues to deal with."

"Yes, it hurts me to think she's been teased," said Rhonda. "Of my three grandchildren, she's the most sensitive."

Though Rhonda and I were known for owning and running a successful hotel, we were, and always would be, mothers and grandmothers. "I've got to get home," said Rhonda. "I'll make some calls to people I know and see what l can find out about Chet Waring."

"And I'll check on Jonny Arno's background and work history. No matter what happens with Chet and Harper, we're going to have to deal with him. And with Brock involved, even on the periphery, it's bound to mean trouble."

I left the hotel shortly after Rhonda and headed home. My husband, Vaughn Sanders, was a well-known actor who was away filming a movie. He came home as often as he could, but he still had a few more weeks before the movie would be wrapped. This was a period when I could accomplish a significant amount of work for the hotel. Tonight would be no exception.

When I walked into our house, our Dachshund, Cindy, greeted me with wiggles and a doggy grin. She certainly couldn't equal a greeting from Vaughn, but with him gone, I'd take it. I lifted her into my arms. She kissed my cheek and nestled against me while I crooned sweet sayings to her.

I set her down on the floor and went to find Robbie. At fourteen, he was growing fast. Most days, he stayed late at school for swim team practice.

I found him sprawled on his bed listening to music on his headphones. He noticed me and sat up. He was the son of my ex and the woman he divorced me for. Robbie had become our child twelve years ago when we adopted him after both his parents were killed in an automobile accident.

Seeing him like this, smiling like my ex, Robert, I was reminded how lucky we were to have him. He was a bright, nice young man who'd been a spoiled two-year-old when he came to live with us. He removed his headphones. "Hi."

"How do you like high school so far?" I asked, sitting on the edge of the bed. "Are you enjoying the swim team? The classes?" A typical boy, he wasn't too forthcoming about his activities. I'd learned to ask open-ended questions.

"They're fine," he said. "Swim team is about the same. Just tougher competition." He flexed his muscles. "I think I'm growing stronger."

I laughed and gave him a quick hug. "Yes, I think you are." I kept my voice light but inside, I felt a stab of regret that time was going by so quickly. Before we knew it, Robbie would be an adult and away at college.

"Hungry?" I asked him. "I thought we'd grill some chicken tonight. Sound okay?"

"Yes, I'm starving," said Robbie. "When's Dad coming home?"

"Not for another couple of weeks. And then he'll be around for a while," I said, already anticipating that time. For all the fame he had achieved in his career, Vaughn loved being at home with us.

"How's the homework situation?" I asked.

"Done," said Robbie, smiling. If a swim team member had failing grades, they were kicked off the team. That rule alone was much more effective than any nagging parent.

"Okay, I'll leave you to your music," I said, rising.

"Thanks, Mom," said Robbie. "Brett and I decided we'd go to the Freshman dance after all. Okay?"

"Yes," I said, surprised. A few short months ago, Robbie wouldn't have ever agreed to go. But he'd started receiving phone calls from girls, making me wonder which girl had caught his eye. "Are you going alone?"

Robbie grinned at me. "Yep."

I smiled to myself. Maybe later I'd get more details.

That night, after doing the dishes, I sat down at my desk in my home office and did an online search on Jonny Arno. He was described as being in his early fifties, a native of Buffalo, New York. He'd studied in Europe at several restaurants, training under a well-known chef in Lyon, France.

I read through another bio of him. He was not married, had no children, and had won several awards for his restaurant in Miami called Chez Michel. Although his bio was impressive, the comments made by some people on a certain social site were not. As Chet and Harper had indicated, Jonny was known for being abusive and difficult to work with. I turned to reviews of his latest cookbook. So many five stars.

After buying an online copy, I read through some of the recipes. As Rhonda had indicated, it would be very difficult to prove that Jonny had stolen some of the recipes from Chet. I realized it had taken a lot of guts for Chet to confront the well-known chef. Even after briefly meeting the young man, I didn't think his claims were about the money. Tomorrow, I'd have a better opportunity to verify that.

I went to check on Robbie, put Cindy outside, and after she came in, I headed to bed.

Slipping under the light blanket, I reached for my ringing cell on the bedside table. Noticing Vaughn's smiling face on the screen, I curled my toes. He still had that effect on me.

"Hey, babe," he said in a sexy drawl I knew was meant to amuse me.

"Hi, sweetheart! How are you?" When we'd first dated, it took me a while to separate the television screen smile and his lines from soap-opera scenes from the true, more intimate ones he gave me.

"I miss you," Vaughn said. "I thought we'd get through this filming sooner, but my co-star is always late and doesn't always know her lines. It's very frustrating. I want to be home with you and the family. I heard from Nell. She and Clint are planning to come for Thanksgiving."

"Yes, I spoke to her as well. I can't wait to see them. I'm still hoping they'll relocate to Florida." I loved Vaughn's daughter, Nell, like my own. She'd always been a big supporter of mine when Vaughn was still recovering from the death of his wife and wasn't sure about marrying again. Ty, Vaughn's son, lived in San Francisco with his wife and family. And though we didn't see him as often as we'd like, we kept in touch.

"What's going on there? Any new suspense at the hotel?" Vaughn teased.

"As a matter of fact, you won't believe what's happening. Brock Goodwin has invested in a new restaurant up the beach from the hotel, and he's claiming it will take a lot of business away from The Beach House Hotel. But the chef, Jonny Arno, is someone who doesn't have a great reputation."

"Brock Goodwin is an ass who just loves to torment you and Rhonda. How can he win this time? Jean-Luc's cooking is known throughout Southwest Florida."

"Here's the twist. A young chef who has been blackballed from working in Miami by Jonny Arno is interested in working for us. Rhonda and I are interviewing him tomorrow. Liz and Angie may hire his girlfriend as a bartender to help expand bar activity with a younger crowd."

"Ah, now that's sounding more like intrigue at the hotel. Vice-President Amelia Swanson isn't involved, is she?"

Chuckling, I said, "So far, she's out of the picture except for continuing to promote the hotel."

"She's put you and Rhonda in danger before. Let's keep her out of this. Okay?"

"I'll try, but we never know when Amelia might need our help," I said, loving the protective tone in his voice.

We talked about Robbie and the swim team and a range of topics and then Vaughn said, "I can't wait to hold you in my arms again. I promise I'll be home as soon as I can."

"Love you," I said, thinking how empty the bed was without him.

CHAPTER THREE

THE NEXT MORNING WHEN I WENT INTO THE HOTEL, I walked into the kitchen to greet Consuela. She was like a mother to me. She and her husband, Manny, had worked for Rhonda before we opened the hotel and became our first staff members after we opened. More than that, they'd replaced the parents neither Rhonda nor I no longer had.

" 'Morning," I said, giving her a kiss on the cheek. "How are you?"

"Busy as always, but I saved you and Rhonda cinnamon rolls, and the coffee is freshly made."

"Has anyone told you what an angel you are? Besides, Manny, I mean."

We chuckled together. Manny had no problem telling anyone how lucky he was to be married to Consuela.

"Rhonda's already in the office. Will you take a sweet roll to her?" Consuela held a plate with two sweet rolls and waited while I poured myself a cup of coffee.

After seeing me off, she went back to overseeing the kitchen for the breakfast meal. Jean-Luc was responsible for dinner and, with the help of a sous chef, lunches.

When I walked into the office, Rhonda looked up at me. "Ah, a sweet roll for me. Thanks."

I handed her one and settled the plate on my desk. Sitting in the morning sipping coffee and eating a sweet roll was often a sort of ritual for us as we began each hectic day.

Rhonda waited until I'd taken a sip of coffee and then said, "I've got some interesting news for you. I talked to a few friends in the hospitality industry in Miami about Jonny Arno. As Chet told us, he did get in touch with people and asked them not to hire Chet. Even so, the people I talked to don't like Jonny and know he's involved in some way with the mafia. They think that's why Jonny moved to the Gulf Coast, to open up a new territory for them."

"The mafia? We don't want anything to do with them," I said, horrified.

"It's not like the old days that my father knew, but kickbacks on suppliers' orders and the like still occur," Rhonda said. "But we don't have to get involved."

"It makes me worried," I said. "Let's just let the new restaurant do their thing, and we'll do ours."

Rhonda studied me. "We'll do what we can to stay out of their way. What about Chet? Do we walk away from him and Harper?"

"No," I quickly said. "He deserves a chance to prove himself with us. Let's interview Chet like any other prospective staff member, and if we approve, we'll send him to Jean-Luc and let him make the decision about hiring him. Still, we need to inform Bernie about the situation."

Bernhard Bruner was our General Manager and was as straight and proper as they come. His wife, Annette, whom he met here at the hotel at her daughter's wedding, worked for us in the dining room and on special events.

"Let's talk to him now while those conversations I had with my friends are still fresh in my mind," said Rhonda.

"We'll record our conversation just for the record," I said. "In case we need it in the future."

"Great idea," said Rhonda. "Let's go."

A few minutes later, Rhonda and I were sitting in front of

Bernie. After I explained the situation with Chet and Harper, Rhonda told him about the conversations she'd had with a few friends in Miami.

"No doubt about it, Jonny Arno is not well-liked and is considered untrustworthy," said Rhonda.

"I did some research," I said. "Jonny grew up in Buffalo, New York, which makes it plausible that he'd have a connection to the mafia because five families still intact are in New York City. The Genoveses and Gambinos are the stronger families. It makes sense they'd work in western New York State as well. A connection to Jonny Arno could be made there."

"We'll continue to conduct our business as normal,' said Bernie. "We've been pretty clear about staying out of anything we consider illegal. There's no reason to adjust to different standards. I refuse to take part in anything like that."

"Like Annie and me," said Rhonda. "The question we have for you is about possibly hiring Chet and making Jonny Arno upset with us. Is that wise? We don't want to hurt our hotel."

Bernie raised an eyebrow. "Is that how you normally choose to conduct your business?"

"No, but we haven't told you everything. Brock Goodwin is part-owner of the new restaurant and is out to get Jean-Luc and ruin our restaurant," I said.

Bernie sat back in his chair and formed a tower with his fingertips. "That puts a different spin on it. Brock, the ass, will gladly play the role agitator that Jonny needs."

"That's what we're afraid of," I said.

"But we won't allow that little bastard to dictate how to run our business," said Rhonda. "That prick isn't going to get away with it."

"Right," I said. "But we don't want anyone else to get hurt. Jean-Luc has worked hard for his excellent reputation."

"Okay, then, let's talk about Chet. I suggest we proceed with a normal interview, and the person with the final decision will be Jean-Luc. He's been talking about the need to hire an additional sous chef. Let's see what he thinks about Chet. By the way, when you do your interview, I'd like to stop by to introduce myself, if you don't mind."

"Okay," said Rhonda. "I want to know what you think about him."

"Angela and Liz have been working on an idea to increase bar revenue with a younger crowd," I said. "They'll interview Chet's girlfriend, Harper, sometime tomorrow."

"It's smart to have their input," said Bernie. "Have them report to me after the interview."

"Of course," I said, both excited and nervous about the challenge of hiring Chet .

That afternoon, Rhonda and I rose to greet Chet when he walked into our office for his interview. I was touched by his appearance. He was wearing what looked like new khaki slacks and a dark gray golf shirt that complemented his dark hair, which still held a trace of moisture from what I assumed was a shower.

"Hello," Chet said with a wide smile.

"We're pleased to have this opportunity to speak with you," I said. "Our General Manager will be stopping in."

"Glad to see you're on time," said Rhonda. "Let's sit at the conference table."

We moved to the table, and all took seats.

From a leather-bound notebook, Chet removed papers and handed each of us his resumé. Glancing at it, I didn't see many new facts until I reached the list of restaurants he'd worked in. Most were located in New York State.

"Was Chez Michel the first restaurant you worked at in Miami?" I asked.

"As a chef, yes," said Chet. "I worked in the kitchen at *Gator's* to see if I liked that more casual side of the business."

"And you decided you didn't?" Rhonda asked.

He shook his head. "I'd rather work hard in a different way to present something creative for guests. It can be difficult, especially to get the timing of trickier recipes down so they're all served at once, but it's worth it. When you're finished, you've created a tasty work of art."

"I love seeing a meal well-plated," I said.

"I want it to look nice, but the real test is in the taste," said Rhonda. "I can still see an image of my grandmother tasting a sauce and trying to decide what else it might need. I do the same thing."

Chet gave her a happy smile. "Me, too. I think of Rosalie when I do it."

"I have a question for you," said Rhonda. "What is the difference between an appetizer and a canapé?

Chet smiled at her. "Hors d'oeuvres are typically served before the meal even begins, while appetizers tend to indicate the beginning of the meal. Canapés are essentially small, open-faced sandwiches made with an edible base of crackers, blinis, bread, or pastry, and served cold. For instance, if you pick up a piece of smoked salmon on a blini from a platter, you have a canapé."

"Why do you want to work here at the hotel with Jean-Luc?" I asked. "When we talked earlier, you made it seem as if you were unsure."

Chet gave us a sheepish look. "I didn't mean to come across that way. I just need to be sure I'm not going to suffer from any problems like I had in Miami. I want to have a clean reputation."

"Jean-Luc, our chef, is an outstanding person," said Rhonda with a defensive tone.

"Oh, I know, I know," said Chet. "He's the kind of man I aspire to be one day. I've just had a very damaging experience and don't want to derail my future altogether."

"I understand," I said. "Now, let's talk about the positives of working with Johnny Arno. You certainly must have learned something from him."

Chet hesitated and then said, "Working for him was a little bit like signing up for a well-known college professor's class and realizing that the teaching would be done by his assistants. Jonny has some very talented people working for him, and I learned a lot from them. One thing Jonny was excellent at was letting his staff do the work. It's the only way to build up experience."

"Like any chef, Jean-Luc is particular about how things are done. He won't tolerate laziness or not following instructions. Can you deal with that?" asked Rhonda.

Chet didn't hesitate. "That's how I'll learn and grow."

Bernie appeared, and after introducing him to Chet, he took a seat at the table and asked some questions of his own. I was surprised when Bernie said, "How many pages of Jonny's new cookbook did you read?"

Chet calmly replied. "All of them."

"Yes, I would have too," said Bernie. "We pride ourselves at The Beach House Hotel by having open discussions about any issues that might arise. It's a congenial group of employees who've been here for some time. We want to keep it that way by ridding ourselves of any who might not fit in."

"Yes, I can see how important that is," said Chet.

"Anyone who's lucky enough to work here understands that," said Bernie getting to his feet. "It was a pleasure to meet you, Chet. Thank you."

After Bernie left, Chet gave Rhonda and me long looks. "I'd really like to work here."

Rhonda and I exchanged looks of approval.

"All right. We'll see if Jean-Luc is available to meet with you," I said.

Rhonda called and after speaking with him, turned to Chet. "It's a good time right now. He's doing dinner prep and might even put you to work."

Chet stood. "Thank you both, very much. I'll go see him now."

"I'll take you to him," said Rhonda.

They left the office, and I wondered if I'd been foolish to think there'd be a problem. Chet seemed pleasant and capable and not one to be pushed around.

CHAPTER FOUR

I LEFT THE OFFICE AND WENT TO THE LOBBY TO SEE HOW the reception desk was doing. The late afternoon was a busy time at the hotel with new guests arriving. After making sure things were going smoothly with people checking in, I walked over to the Lobby Bar to see the situation there. The bar was active with guests wanting refreshments before the evening festivities. Drinks and snacks were also available at the pool and at the beach, but for those not in swimsuits, the Lobby Bar was a place to be seen and to meet up with friends.

I was surprised to find Harper sitting there and went over to her.

"Afternoon. How are you today?" I asked her.

"Fine, thank you. Just waiting to hear from Chet about how things went with the interview with Jean-Luc. He texted me that he was about to talk with him now."

"He's an outstanding candidate," I said. "But Jean-Luc will make the decision as to whether he's hired. How about you? Are you still interested in working here at the hotel?"

"Yes," said Harper. "I've been watching the activity and understand wanting to draw more young people in."

"Rhonda's daughter and mine will interview you tomorrow. If they haven't been in touch with you yet, they will be."

"Thanks so much," said Harper. "I hope it all works out." Her cell phone rang. She answered and listened. Then spoke to us. "Chet says Jean-Luc is putting him to work right away and he'll meet me at the motel."

"That's an excellent sign," I said. "Jean-Luc demands the best from people, but he isn't like Jonny Arno."

"It has been a very difficult time for Chet and me," said Harper. "How can someone wield that much power?"

"You should be aware that Jonny Arno is associated with a new restaurant up the beach from us. Both you and Chet will have to be careful," I said. "I'd hate for any problems to arise because we hired him."

"I understand," said Harper, her expression serious.

"Okay. You should be hearing from our daughters, either Liz Bowen or Angela Smythe. I have a feeling you three will get along very nicely."

I waved to the bartender and left feeling happy about things.

As I was settling in my chair in the office, Rhonda appeared wearing a satisfied smile.

"Jean-Luc was very impressed with Chet's attitude. He put him right to work helping with dinner tonight. Chet was more than happy to step in. I think it's going to work out very well."

"I spoke with Harper," I said. "She wants to work here, and I think our daughters are going to like the way she already agrees on the idea of increasing the bar business."

"One point that Jean-Luc stressed to Chet was that we're not competing with anyone. We don't have to. We've successfully established the kind of hotel we run and the restaurant he oversees. The result of that is the responsibility to keep to those high standards."

"Well said." I gave my partner a steady look. "I hope others will respect that."

"I say we keep Brock Goodwin away from the hotel as much as possible," said Rhonda. "We'll notify security and the dining room that he's no friend."

"I think that's smart, though I believe most already know

that," I said. Brock Goodwin had no morals and no love for us. He'd proved it over and over. This time we'd try to stop him before he did damage.

There was a knock on the door. Lorraine Grace, now married to Angela's father-in-law, Arthur Smythe, opened it and peered inside, "Do you have time to talk to me?"

"Sure. Come in," I said, standing and pulling a chair closer to Rhonda and me.

Lorraine lowered herself into the chair and took a moment to speak. "I've just had a call from Amelia Swanson."

"Oh, no," groaned Rhonda. "What does she want now?"

"It's not for a wedding. It's a private dinner for the Italian Ambassador in New York City. After his time is up as the Ambassador, he and his wife are hoping to settle here in the U.S. part-time. Specifically, in Florida. And Amelia wants him to visit Sabal. Because her sister, Lindsay, is married to Jean-Luc, it seems only right for Lindsay to show them around the area. First, Amelia wants us to welcome them in grand style."

"When is this visit?" I asked, suspicious of the timing.

"Tomorrow night. It's the only time the Ambassador could get away within a reasonable amount of time. I have him and his family booked in the Presidential Suite."

"Is the private dining room available?" I asked.

"That's not the problem," said Lorraine. "The issue is that he wants an authentic Italian meal. Amelia told him about Rhonda's cooking ..." She let her voice drift away.

I turned to Rhonda. "Can you do that? What about Jean-Luc's pride?"

"That's why I need your help," said Lorraine. "Amelia wants to show off Jean-Luc's skill the next day at lunch. She knows her brother-in-law is sensitive but feels that providing a special lunch will give him a chance to shine."

"I'll tell you what," said Rhonda after a few moments. "I'll have Chet help me with the main course. He can start early in the morning, so it won't disrupt any work in the kitchen later in the day. The staff can prepare salad and dessert as usual under Jean-Luc's supervision. I'll do my usual antipasto."

"That will make it seem more like a joint effort," I said. "Thank you, Rhonda."

"Who is going to tell Jean-Luc?" Lorraine said.

Both Lorraine and Rhonda turned to me.

"Annie, you know you're better at being diplomatic than I am," said Rhonda.

"It needs to come from one of you, not me," said Lorraine.

Sighing heavily, I said, "Okay. But I'll have to think of a way to say it without hurting Jean-Luc's feelings. Amelia always gives us a task we don't want."

"At least this one won't be dangerous," said Rhonda, chuckling.

"Just one more thing," said Lorraine. "Because Annette and I'll be busy overseeing a rehearsal dinner for that evening, I'll need you, Ann, to oversee the Italian Ambassador's dinner as you often do."

"What else?" I asked, letting out a sigh.

"That's it," said Lorraine. "The rest is up to you two to decide."

Rhonda and I exchanged glances. The hotel business was full of surprises.

Telling myself not to be nervous, I headed to the kitchen to talk to Jean-Luc. Preparations were well underway for the dinner crowd. I stood quietly by watching the interaction among the kitchen staff, delighted to see how well Chet seemed to be fitting in.

Jean-Luc noticed me and walked over. "Hi, Ann, Checking

on our new employee? He's completed the paperwork and is now helping in the kitchen. He reminds me of myself at that age. Willing to work at anything to learn."

"I'm glad to hear it, though that's not why I'm here. Amelia Swanson has a special request for all of us," I said.

Jean-Luc frowned. "That can only mean trouble. I know my sister-in-law."

"This request seems quite simple and a test to see if Chet will become a real part of the team." I told him what we had in mind, watching his face change expressions until he finally nodded.

"Okay. Rhonda and Chet can do two of the courses for dinner. The other menu items will be taken care of by my staff. I will handle their special lunch the following day, but it won't be with Italian food. It will showcase some of my favorite things."

"Yes, that's exactly what they want," I said, breathing a sigh of relief. Somehow, Amelia Swanson always got her way.

I started to walk away and turned back. "Let's give the Ambassador and his wife some outstanding canapés, as well."

Jean-Luc turned away, but not before I saw a look of disappointment on his face. He was a proud man and a decent one, too. I'd leave it to Lindsay to help soothe his feelings.

Rhonda was making a list of items to buy for the menu she was planning. "I'll go to my specialty store for some of these things this evening. Chet can pick them up later so we can talk about preparing the meal. If this doesn't make him decide he's made a mistake by coming on board with us, nothing will."

"But that's how running a hotel is—dealing with one crisis after another. And if he's going to be part of our staff, he must learn it," I said. "We did everything ourselves to get the hotel up and running. And we still have to be flexible and willing to do any job to keep it going."

"Especially when we deal with so many high-profile guests," agreed Rhonda.

My cell phone rang. I nudged Rhonda. "Amelia Swanson."

"Hello, Madame Vice-President," I said politely. "How are you?"

"Did you get the message about the Ambassador's visit to Florida? Is he staying in the Presidential Suite?" she asked without exchanging pleasantries.

I realized she was busy and quickly answered. "Yes, they'll be in the Presidential Suite with a special, authentic Italian dinner and a Jean-Luc luncheon the next day. I suggest you talk to Jean-Luc, though."

"I will. I promise. Thanks for your help. I don't know what I'd do without the two of you stepping in to help me from time to time," she said. "Thanks a million."

The call ended, and I turned to Rhonda. "Amelia says thanks, she doesn't know what she'd do without our help."

"Let's keep that in mind," said Rhonda, "when it comes our turn to ask her for help."

A shudder ran through me. "I hope that doesn't happen anytime soon."

"Aw, I was just saying it, Annie. I don't think it will come to that. We can get rid of Brock Goodwin by ourselves."

"And Jonny?"

"That's another story," Rhonda said. "But I have friends of my own. Friends from the neighborhood."

I grimaced, sensing trouble was coming.

CHAPTER FIVE

AFTER SEEING ROBBIE OFF TO SCHOOL AND SAYING goodbye to Cindy, I headed for the hotel. Though it was early, I wanted to make sure Chet was on board with the day's special activity. It would also give me time to walk on the beach.

When I arrived at the hotel, I said hello to Consuela and peeked into the kitchen. Chet was busy chopping tomatoes for the gravy he was preparing. Later, he and Rhonda would create the main course.

"How are you doing?" I asked him.

"Good," he said. "An authentic gravy has to be cooked all day, so I'm glad I could get it started. Rhonda told me that unusual requests like this come up from time to time."

"Yes, that's part of the hotel business with different guests coming and going with demands for special service. I'm glad you decided to accept Jean-Luc's job offer. We still have more paperwork for you to sign today. Stop by the office when you're free."

I looked around the kitchen at the staff members who were busy preparing for the breakfast rush. In addition to our guests, the dining room was open to locals and visitors. A meal at The Beach House Hotel was a treat for anyone who loved tasty food.

I went back to Consuela and chatted with her for a moment before grabbing a cup of coffee and a cinnamon roll.

A few minutes later, still enjoying my coffee, I looked up as Bernie knocked and entered the office.

" 'Morning! How are you?"

"A bit frustrated. Have you seen the local newspaper? Terri Thomas at the Sabal *Daily News* has written an article headlined, *"A Battle Between Two Greats."*

"Wha-a-a-t?" I said, taking the paper from him.

Terri had interviewed Jonny Arno and written about his new restaurant opening up. She then segued into a piece comparing Jonny and Jean-Luc, claiming that a battle for adulation for the two chefs was about to happen between the two of them.

I sat back in my chair and looked up at Bernie. "I wish she hadn't created her story that way. Though it might seem like a smart idea to increase business for both restaurants, we don't want anything to do with Jonny Arno. Not after knowing the kind of man he is and the connections he has."

"My thoughts exactly," said Bernie. "We don't want to appear as if we need that kind of publicity. We're an upscale place with an excellent chef and excellent service. For all the enthusiastic speculation, I doubt that will be the case with Osteria Arno, especially if people like Brock Goodwin are associated with it."

Rhonda appeared, and we showed her the article.

"Battle, my ass," she sputtered. "Jean-Luc's reputation doesn't need to be tarnished by some imagined battle. Terri should have talked to us before publishing something like this."

"I have a feeling that Terri was contacted by someone on Jonny's team. Someone we might know."

"I'm going to wring Brock's neck," Rhonda said.

"I think we should say nothing about the article, not respond to it in any way," said Bernie. "As we agreed earlier, we don't need to. I've got a meeting right now. Good luck with the Ambassador. I'm planning on welcoming him to the hotel and will try to stop by the cocktail hour to speak to him."

"Thanks," I said. "Amelia wants us to make him feel especially welcome."

Bernie left, and I turned to Rhonda. "How's the cooking going?"

"Chet is off to a satisfactory start. The sauce smells like my grandmother's kitchen," she said with a pleased look. "The veal I ordered will be delivered shortly, along with the Castelvetrano olives and other specialty items."

"I'm going to call Tropical Fleurs and have them create a table centerpiece for us, incorporating the red, green, and white colors of the Italian flag. Something subtle, but nice. And as soon as Annette comes in, I'll arrange for her to supervise the event staff for cocktails and dinner."

"It sounds like things are under control. I'm glad because I promised Angie I'd go to a teacher's meeting with her this afternoon to discuss Sally Kate's issues at school. I told Angie I'd pay for a special tutor."

"That's terrific," I said. "Sally Kate is an adorable child. I would hate to see her self-esteem suffer."

"Yes," said Rhonda. "She's a bright little girl, and I don't want her to think otherwise."

"Rather than call someone at Tropical Fleurs, I think I'll go downtown to visit them. Danielle and her staff are very creative, and I want to talk to her about something unusual not only as a centerpiece for dinner, but for something special in the Presidential Suite."

"When you get back, we'll have our usual pre-wedding meeting with Lorraine and her staff.," said Rhonda. "I heard the groom is the son of some media mogul, and we need to make sure everything goes smoothly."

"Yes, I think his father is a bigwig at Apple. The bride is the one I worry about. If the groom is smart, he'll simply show up and just say 'I do'."

Rhonda and I laughed together. If it were only that simple.

It was such a lovely day that I decided to walk the few blocks to Main Street. As I did, I was reminded of what a beautiful place Sabal was. Condos and large homes lined the beach and filled a block or two inland. Main Street consisted of interesting, upscale shops whose windows held treasures of all kinds. Pots of flowers stood outside doors adding color to the palm tree-lined street.

Passing a little alleyway, I thought of André's, a French restaurant I adored. I vowed the next time Vaughn was at home, we'd have a meal there.

Tropical Fleurs was a couple of doors down, and I stopped to look at a display in the window, created, no doubt, for one of the businesses in town. Store window displays were rotated throughout the day,

When I went inside, Danielle, the store manager, greeted me. "Hi, Ann! What brings you here?"

"I have a special dinner tonight at the hotel, and I'm wondering if you can create something unique for our visitor. It's an Italian dinner theme, and it's to be a small group."

"I know you can't give me any more information than that but let me ask how formal the dinner will be?" said Danielle.

"It will be very formal," I said, unable to tell her who the dinner was for. One of the reasons The Beach House Hotel had done well from the beginning was our policy of providing our guests privacy. We never mentioned who was staying with us, and our staff signed NDA agreements preventing them from disclosing that information.

"When do you need it?" Danielle asked.

"Delivered by five o'clock,' I answered. "I'd like something both tropical and natural with the red, green, and white of Italy's flag. Something that acknowledges Italy but showcases the flowers of Florida. And we'd like to have dark green candles, perhaps surrounded with a bit of the pieces in the arrangement. We need something similar for the Presidential Suite."

Danielle placed a finger on her cheek thoughtfully. "I think I have what you want. I'll put something together and text you a shot of it for your approval."

"That would be lovely," I said. "I trust you to do your usual excellent work; I just wanted to make sure you understood how important this is."

"I saw Terri's column in the paper this morning," said Danielle. "How does Jean-Luc feel about being in a contest with Jonny Arno?"

"We haven't spoken to him about it. Rhonda, Bernie, and I aren't interested in competing. We'll continue to carry on as we always have."

"I hear both good and bad things about Osteria Arno. But to be truthful, we did get the contract to provide flowers for them. It's a strange arrangement with them. They forced us to give them a percentage off our normal prices. For an initial time, we can work around it, but still I thought it was pushy on their part."

"Who did you negotiate with?" I asked.

"The manager is a man named Tony Costello. I was surprised when I learned the name of the restaurant. It's similar to the title of the cookbook he recently released."

"I think it must be a matter of pride," I said. "I've heard Jonny has a big ego."

"I normally wouldn't say anything about another customer, but Brock Goodwin stopped by to tell me I owe him for mentioning my name to Tony Costello. How anyone can stand him is beyond me. You'd think he was the mayor of New York, not the president of his neighborhood association."

"He's a thorn in my side and Rhonda's. He has been since before we opened. I don't want to say too much, but I'd be cautious working with the new restaurant he's involved with." I wanted to say so much more but didn't. I didn't want any fighting to begin with him or the people behind Jonny's new restaurant. The idea terrified me.

That afternoon, after Rhonda and I met with Lorraine regarding the wedding, I was pleased to see Liz and Angela come into our office.

"Hi, Mom! We're here to interview Harper Lewis. We'll report to you after our meeting," said Liz proudly.

"Wonderful," I said, getting to my feet and hugging each of them. "I have to go home and change clothes for the evening's activities. But I'll be back in time to talk to you after you speak to Harper. Rhonda is busy putting together some food for tonight's important dinner. It's an upscale Italian dinner like her grandmother used to serve."

"I hope there are leftovers," teased Angie. "I know what she's making."

I studied small, dark-haired Angela standing next to my tall, blond daughter and was grateful that they'd gone from being freshman roommates at Boston University to life-long best friends. It was through our daughters that Rhonda and I became friends.

At home, I stripped my clothes off, freshened up, and put on one of my standard dresses used for social events like this— a simple, black sleeveless sheath with a chunky gold and diamond necklace, solitaire diamond earrings, and comfortable black sandals.

The doorbell rang, and I went to usher in Liana Sousa, who helped us out from time to time. She was always willing to see that Robbie was fed a healthy dinner and was comfortably settled for the night before I came home from hosting events at the hotel.

"Hi, how are you?" I asked her. "Thanks for coming at the last minute. I know you're busy with college classes and an active social life."

"College would never have happened if you hadn't paid for my schooling," Liana said. "I'm happy to help in return." Vaughn and I had decided to pay her on a regular monthly basis in order to retain her for babysitting services anytime we needed it. The plan had worked well for all of us.

Cindy gamboled at Liana's feet, wanting attention.

Liana picked her up and hugged her.

"Robbie will be home after swim practice," I said. "I've arranged for a ride home. I thought you could make him his favorite tacos for dinner."

"That's easy. I'll take care of it. I froze ingredients for them the last time I was here," said Liana. "I know Mr. Sanders likes them too."

"Yes, he does."

"When is he coming home?" Liana asked. "I'll make another batch of sauce and fillings for him."

"He won't be through filming for another couple of weeks," I said, inwardly sighing. The last few weeks of any filming seemed to take forever. For everyone.

CHAPTER SIX

WHEN I RETURNED TO THE HOTEL, ANGIE, LIZ, AND Rhonda were sitting in the office.

"How did the interview with Harper go?" I asked them.

"Very well," said Liz. "Harper is a perfect fit for the program that Angie and I are working on."

"She's really excited about the idea of blending an older crowd with younger people. She told us she's spent time in the bar almost every day for a week, checking things out," said Angie.

"She's taken several marketing classes and wants to work with us on a variety of things but will gladly tend bar until we're ready to focus on them." Liz laughed. "She also understands about our having family responsibilities. She's the oldest of five children. All her younger siblings are boys."

"I know you think she and Chet are together," said Angie. "But they're not. We found out they're just friends who are temporarily sharing a motel room."

"Interesting," I said. "I like them both."

"I'm excited that it'll be up to Liz and me to carry on with the hotel after you and Mom decide to retire," said Angie. "We've talked about it for years, but this project seems like a fresh start to our involvement now that our families are complete."

"Yes, four are enough for me," said Liz. "I want each of them to feel special."

"They *are* special," said Rhonda with feeling. Like me, she'd wanted to have lots of children but couldn't. Rhonda had only Angie for years until she married Will and had been surprised to have two more children with him.

"Is Harper working the bar tonight?" I asked.

"Yes," said Angie. "We know the hotel is busy with the special dinner and the wedding, and with Chet already working here, Harper was delighted to be asked to begin."

"She filled out some paperwork and will go to the HR office tomorrow to take care of the rest," Liz said, rising. "I need to go home. The Ts have dentist appointments."

I chuckled. 'The Ts' is what we sometimes called the triplets rather than speaking all three names. Olivia, Emma, and Noah.

Angie left with Liz , and Rhonda and I sat a moment before leaving to go to the front of the hotel to greet the Ambassador and his wife. From the first time guests arrived at the hotel, Rhonda and I made every effort to greet them ourselves. It was part of the vision we had to change Rhonda's seaside estate into a small, upscale hotel that welcomed guests as if they were arriving to our home. And with guests like the Ambassador, it was something we felt we needed to do.

"How's the cooking coming?" I asked Rhonda as we left the office a few minutes later.

"I'm impressed with Chet. He's very organized. And we agree on special seasoning."

"Any reaction from Jean-Luc about the two of you in charge of this dinner?" I asked.

Rhonda shrugged. "We're being very careful to stay out of the way of the other staff. I'm sure Amelia had a positive talk with him. He's so happily married to her sister, Jean-Luc would do anything to please them both."

"Few people can say no to Amelia," I said. We never wanted to upset Jean-Luc enough to leave. Aside from being a talented chef, he'd become a dear friend.

We stood at the top of the hotel's main entry staircase and waited while a white limousine pulled up to the front.

"Here goes," said Rhonda, descending the staircase quickly, her rose caftan flowing behind her.

I kept pace, and when the driver opened the back door of the limo, Ambassador Enrico Ferrara emerged. He was a heavy-set man of average height with black hair and a mustache.

He turned and helped a tall, attractive, blonde woman out of the car and stood a moment while she fussed with her brown-linen dress before turning to face us.

"Welcome to The Beach House Hotel," I said, stepping forward to shake hands.

"Enjoy your stay here," Rhonda added, smiling at them. "I'm Rhonda Grayson, and this is my business partner, Ann Sanders."

The Ambassador introduced himself and his wife, Catarina, and they both indicated a beautiful young woman exiting the limo. "This is our daughter, Philippa."

Blond like her mother, tall, and with an alluring figure in a short, blue sleeveless sundress that complimented her, Philippa said hello as if it were a duty, nothing more.

I saw a frown cross her mother's face, but nothing was said about her daughter's lack of excitement.

Without missing a beat, Enrico said, "Your hotel comes with a high recommendation from the vice-president. I look forward to our visit, though it's shorter than I would wish."

"We're delighted to have you and your family," I said. "We've placed you in the Presidential Suite."

"Excellent," Enrico said. "I'm sure we'll find it very suitable." He held out his hand. "Come, Catarina."

Rhonda led them up the stairs.

I turned to Philippa. "Let me show you to where to go."

Philippa made a face. "Thanks. My parents made me come with them. I was supposed to stay in New York with friends."

"I understand the visit here will be a short one. Perhaps you'll be back with your friends soon," I said.

Philippa shook her head. "They want me to return to Italy with them in a couple of weeks to take care of some family business. An old-fashioned marriage idea."

From the top of the stairs, Enrico turned to us. "Philippa, are you coming?"

"Be right there, Papa," said Philippa and emitted a long sigh.

I walked with her up the stairs, wondering how Liz would've acted if I'd tried to arrange a marriage for her. No, I didn't need to wonder, I knew she'd be furious.

Next to me, Philippa moved with grace, though I could tell by the thrust of her chin she was still feeling defiant.

At the top of the stairs, we entered the hotel, and I led Philippa across the lobby to the staircase leading to the private Presidential Suite.

She turned to me. "Can you show me to your beach?"

"Of course," I said. "If you come this way, you'll see the pool area and beyond it the beach. The hotel provides chairs and offers some sports equipment."

"Thank you," said Phillippa. "I'm supposed to meet a friend from New York there shortly. No worries. I can find my way around from here. I appreciate your time."

Satisfied that she seemed happier, I left her and went to the office to talk to Rhonda. She needed to be warned of the situation between Philippa and her parents. I had a feeling that family problems would end up in our lap.

In the office, Rhonda told me that Enrico had requested space for two more dinner guests, making it ten instead of eight. "I told him no problem. We have plenty of food."

"I had an interesting talk with their daughter," I said, filling her in on the details of my conversation with Philippa.

"It does seem strange," said Rhonda. Her eyes lit. "Unless it's something dictated by one of the mafia families in Italy."

"Maybe so," I said, uneasy about the idea. Every time we did something for Amelia Swanson, we ended up in trouble.

As if she'd read my mind, Rhonda said, "I hope we don't end up in another mess caused by our dear vice-president."

"Me, too. Vaughn is very understanding of my time commitment to the hotel, but he doesn't like it when Amelia pulls us into situations that could put us at risk in any way."

"Thank God, the Ambassador's family is here for just a couple of nights," said Rhonda. "You'll have to pay close attention at dinner, though, and listen for any details that might help us understand the situation."

"Private dinners at our hotel are known for our being discreet, but that doesn't mean I won't be listening to what's being said."

"Far better it's you than me who handles these dinners. You know if I heard something I didn't like, I'd react before thinking," said Rhonda.

It was true. Oftentimes, it was necessary for me to pretend I hadn't heard a secret or some other piece of information no one else should know about.

"I've got to go," said Rhonda "We're sending wine and a special welcome basket to the Presidential Suite. I want to make sure it's just right. I'm calling Annette now to tell her about the two additional guests."

"Thanks," I said. "It's early but she and I don't like any last minute surprises."

I walked to the Social Events office where Lorraine's wedding business was located, along with offices for Lorraine's assistant, Lauren, and an office for Annette, who handled a lot of our social events not associated with an in-house wedding.

Lorraine looked up from her desk and waved as I went to Annette's cubicle. She was on the phone. I waited until she was through and then asked her about the staff for tonight's private dinner.

"We're all set. The bartender and two waitresses are ready to go. I just got off the phone with Rhonda , I'll hire one more waitress to handle the enlarged group. I know how important these dinners are."

"Thanks. I understand you'll be working the wedding this weekend. It's another important event for us."

"Oh, yes, I know. The mother-of-the-bride has made that abundantly clear." Annette shook her head. "I personally don't care how much money someone makes, or how important someone thinks they are, there's no need to be obnoxious about it."

"I'm sorry. Some of our weddings are so sweet, others, not so much."

"Yeah, this is one of those others," complained Annette.

I laughed, but I knew Annette would be unerringly polite and competent, so I could only give her a pat on the back and say, "Thanks."

I went to the private dining room, one of my favorite rooms at the hotel. Soon after we opened, we realized we needed a place where meetings and dinners, sometimes secret ones, could be held. We turned a conference room into a luxurious dining room that could be used for both.

I opened the door and went inside.

The palest of gold silk covered the walls of the room, giving it a touch of warmth that enhanced the long, wooden, dining room table surrounded by carved wooden chairs with seafoam green velvet seats. The matching sideboard had many uses, including storage of extra supplies. A large mirror with a gold frame hung above it, reflecting the image of palm trees outside the window.

A warm walnut wood bar sat at the far end of the room, with enough space between it and the dining room table for people to gather. We had the furnishings and equipment to remove the dining table and replace it with round tables for a less formal affair.

This evening, a crisp white tablecloth covered the long table. Gold-rimmed ivory chinaware, sparkling crystal glasses, and shiny silverware were in place for eight.

A waitress arrived with two additional place settings and quickly rearranged the table. A houseman appeared with two extra chairs. I checked my watch. Danielle from Tropical Fleurs should deliver the table centerpiece soon. The photo she'd texted looked fabulous.

When I heard her outside the door, I opened it to let her in. Usually, one of her helpers delivered the flowers, but on special occasions, Danielle herself brought them.

Danielle entered and placed a stunning centerpiece on the table. Pieces of driftwood on a long, green dish were covered with a number of red and white orchids with added touches of greenery.

"Oh, it's even lovelier than the photo," I said. "I don't know how you do it. A bit of the tropics and Italy too. Thanks so much."

"I wanted to do something that would do justice to this room. It's a favorite of mine."

"I love it, too," I said. "Thanks for your help."

Danielle departed, and I left to go to my office to wait until it was time for me to welcome people to the dinner. Having a few minutes alone in my office was a way to prepare myself to greet my guests and spend an evening with them.

CHAPTER SEVEN

I STOOD BESIDE ANNETTE AT THE DOOR OF THE PRIVATE dining room ready to greet our guests. In addition to the Ambassador, his wife, and daughter, the mayor of Sabal and two businessmen in the area, partners in a real estate company, were due to attend. A couple who resided in nearby Marco Island had also been invited, along with the two extra mystery guests who'd been added at the last minute.

"I like these smaller groups," said Annette. "It's easier to get to know them. Sorry I won't be able to stay tonight, but the wedding party is a demanding one, and I can't leave Lorraine handling the dinner alone. Not with that mother-of-the-bride."

"I understand," I said. "It's how the business goes. We all have to pitch in whenever we can."

"Rhonda is helping to prepare the food?" Annette asked.

"Yes, it's going to be delicious. She and our new sous-chef are doing it together using old family recipes."

Annette chuckled. "My mouth is watering."

We looked up as the mayor of Sabal, Helena Naylor, arrived. Of medium height, with blond hair pulled back into a bun, she was an attractive woman with sparkling blue eyes that shone with intelligence and a sense of humor.

A friend to both Annette and me, she gave us each a hug. "I'm pleased to be here. It will be a chance for me to encourage Italian visitors to our area."

"Other business contacts have been invited," I said. "People I don't really know."

We turned as two men arrived dressed in matching dark summer suits. Their crisp white shirts and red ties seemed appropriate for the evening.

"Ah, you must be the Luna brothers, Gil and Leon," said Annette smiling at them.

Silently blessing her for giving me their names, I stepped forward. "Welcome to The Beach House Hotel. I haven't had need for a real estate agent, but I understand you're active in the community."

Gil, the older-looking man, said, "Sabal is a place where everyone wants to be. It provides us a reliable business."

Leon, his younger brother, handed us a business card with the information for Destiny Real Estate on it. "We'd like to be able to work with you on providing your guests with our information."

Smiling, I took the card and simply said, "Thank you." We didn't get involved in making recommendations for businesses like theirs.

The men went inside and over to the bar where Helena stood talking to the bartender, an older man we often used for events like this.

A couple arrived and announced they were Marco and Bridget Morena.

"Welcome to The Beach House Hotel," I said. "It's lovely to see you."

"Thank you," said Bridget. "We recently moved here, and I've heard so much about The Beach House Hotel that I'm very glad to be included."

I started to speak when I noticed Brock Goodwin and another man walking toward us.

Annette saw the shock in my face and quickly intervened to help usher Bridget and Marco inside.

"What are you doing here?" I asked Brock quietly.

I studied his companion whom I recognized from photos taken when he was much younger. He carried himself with an air of self-importance. What had once been dark brown hair was obviously dyed a lighter shade and did nothing to enhance his florid face, which spoke of overindulgence. There was a sleaziness to him I found revolting when he winked at me.

"I'd like to introduce you to Jonny Arno," Brock said. "My business partner."

Jonny shrugged. "Business partner, Brock. That's a bit of a stretch."

Blushing, Brock continued. "We're here tonight for the dinner to be held in Ambassador Ferrara's honor. I told his staff that as President of the Neighborhood Association, I should be included along with the most important chef in the area."

Annette reappeared, saving me from saying something ugly to him.

" 'Evening, Brock," she said in a cool voice.

"I'd like you to meet Jonny Arno, the new, best chef in the area. Or he soon will be," said Brock, clapping Jonny on the back. "This is Ann Sanders, one of the owners, and Annette Bernhard, a staff member."

A fleeting smile crossed Jonny's fleshy face and then he held out his hand. "Nice to meet you both."

"Won't you come this way," said Annette. "The Ambassador and his family will soon join us."

The three of them went inside and I stood a moment quietly seething. Brock Goodwin was a master at interjecting himself into our business. *Damn it!*

"Are you alright?" Annette asked, rejoining me.

"No, I'm not. But I'll do my best not to show it," I said.

"Brock Goodwin is understandably upsetting," said Annette. "Here are the Ambassador and his wife now."

Enrico and Caterina walked toward us looking regal. Enrico was in a navy suit and wore the Order of Merit of the Italian Republic on the chest of his suitcoat. Caterina looked fabulous in a long, golden dress whose simple lines spoke of high quality.

"Welcome to your special dinner," I said. "Your guests await you." I looked around. "Is Philippa going to be joining you this evening?"

"Yes," said Catarina firmly. "She's dressing now."

"Please follow me," I said.

When we walked into the dining room, the seven people there turned and began to applaud.

With a delighted smile, Enrico bobbed his head and held out a hand to his wife.

The two of them stood there a moment and then walked over to the group standing by the bar.

I went outside hoping to catch sight of Philippa.

A few minutes later, Philippa hurried across the lobby over to me.

"Sorry I'm late. My mother's furious, but I was with my friend and forgot the time. How do I look?"

"Stunning," I said honestly. "That dress is perfect."

Philippa was wearing a sleeveless red dress that fell to her calves and showed her lovely curves. Her blond hair was swept up in a clump behind her head and showed off the diamonds she wore in her ears. The afternoon sun had already kissed her smooth cheeks with color, accentuating her sparkling brown eyes.

Philippa rubbed her lips together to smooth the red gloss she'd applied and straightened. "Okay. I'm ready."

I opened the door, and Philippa swept inside attracting the attention of the others. When I noticed a leer cross Brock's face, I chastened myself for not warning Philippa about

Brock's behavior.

He stepped forward to greet her, but she walked right by him without giving him any attention. The look of disappointment on Brock's face was laughable as Philippa continued over to her father.

Enrico wrapped an arm around Philippa and gazed at her with a father's pride.

A waitress wearing a black skirt and white blouse passed by with a tray of canapés that looked delicious. Our guests thought so too as they quickly helped themselves to some.

Annette came up to me. "I'll leave you now. The staff is here and ready."

"Thank you. I'll see to the rest. Good luck with the rehearsal dinner."

I stood quietly to the side making sure no glasses were left empty, and food was being properly offered.

I noticed Enrico and Jonny Arno having a conversation and wondered what they might be talking about. Brock joined them, and Enrico soon left the group.

Helena and Catarina were in conversation. Philippa stood by looking bored. When she noticed Brock headed her way, she turned toward her mother and joined in.

After being given the signal from the kitchen, I spoke up. "Please, everyone, be seated for dinner. You will find place cards with your name on it at the table." I'd made sure that Brock was not seated next to either Philippa or her mother.

Guests took their seats, and while they studied the event's menu, two waitresses poured water, either still or sparkling as each guest wished.

A knock on the door was followed by Bernie's appearance.

"Hello, everyone. As General Manager of The Beach House Hotel, it is my pleasure to welcome you to a very special evening in honor of Ambassador Ferrara and his lovely family.

Enjoy a touch of Italy prepared especially for you."

Bernie and I shook hands, and then he left.

At another signal, I opened the door, and a waiter rolled in a cart carrying the first course of individual plates of antipasti. Each one I inspected held a small selection of cheeses, olives, salami, peppers, and other pressed meats artfully arranged.

When the antipasti were set down in front of our guests, their looks of anticipation meant we'd done an excellent job.

"*Buon Appetito!*" I said, raising my water glass from the sideboard in a salute.

"*Grazie mille*! This looks fabulous," said Enrico, lifting his glass of red wine.

I was happy we were off to a pleasing start, notwithstanding a look of concern on Jonny Arno's face.

The next course was penne Bolognese. I spoke quietly to Enrico as it was being served, "This is made especially for you, as requested, and is from old family recipes. Enjoy."

I watched as Enrico took his first bite, closed his eyes, and let out an audible sigh of pleasure. "*Delizioso.*"

Jonny Arno squirmed in his chair.

More wine was poured as each guest took their time savoring the meal.

By the time the next course arrived, conversation was flowing easily between the diners.

"Another family specialty to remind you of home," I told Enrico. "Veal marsala just as you requested."

After all the veal dishes were served, Enrico lifted his fork. "My favorite." He took a bite of the tender veal topped with a wine, garlic, and mushroom sauce and lifted his napkin to one eye. "Like Mama's."

Catarina smiled at him from across the table. "*Si.* Like your mother's dish."

When Tiramisu was served with coffee and tea, the quiet in

the room attested to its deliciousness.

Enrico signaled for me to come closer. "I want to thank the chef for this fabulous meal."

"Actually, three people and other staff made this meal possible."

"Bring them out, please. I want to thank them personally."

"I'll let them know," I said, and left the room to go to the kitchen.

"How's it going?" Rhonda asked wearing an apron and standing by a stove.

"Very, very well. I think Enrico even cried over the veal marsala. Now he wants to thank the three chefs who created the meal."

"Okay," said Rhonda. "Chet, Jean-Luc, and me?"

"Yes, but I must warn you that Jonny Arno and Brock Goodwin were the two last-minute guests added to the dinner party."

"You've got to be shittin' me," said Rhonda. "Just what we need."

"Let's pretend they aren't there. Just get the other two and come with me. We'll make this awkward situation become to our benefit."

Rhonda took off her apron and went to find Chet and Jean-Luc.

Tossing dirty aprons aside, Chet and Jean-Luc followed Rhonda and me to the private dining room.

As we entered the room, everyone clapped.

"*Eccellente*," shouted Enrico. "I don't know how you did it, but this meal tasted exactly how my mother and grandmother used to make it."

"Thank you," I said. "It's thanks to my business partner, Rhonda Grayson, our chef, Jean-Luc Rodin, and our new sous chef, Chet Waring."

"It was a pleasure to present this meal to you, Mr. Ambassador," said Rhonda.

While people clapped and commented, I noticed a look of shock cross Philippa's face as she gazed at Chet. Then it quickly disappeared. I turned to Chet. His cheeks were pink, and he looked as surprised as Philippa, unaware that Jonny Arno was glaring at him.

Then, with a last little bow, Rhonda, Chet, and Jean-Luc left.

I turned at the sound of Jonny Arno getting to his feet. "I'm here to announce the opening of my new restaurant, Osteria Arno, and to formally ask for Ambassador Ferrara's support."

The room grew quiet. What had been a sweet, family affair shifted to a scene of uneasiness as the Ambassador gave Jonny a stern look. "This isn't the time for business."

I quickly tried to recover. "Thank you and everyone else for coming tonight to celebrate Ambassador Ferrara and his family. Enjoy the rest of your evening."

Everyone got to their feet, essentially ending the event.

Obviously unhappy, Jonny approached me. "We could've started off being friends."

"There's no reason not to be friends," I said, ignoring his threatening tone.

"I intend to be the best, have the most successful restaurant in the area," said Jonny, giving me a challenging look. "And I don't need a certain sous chef to make that happen,"

Forcing myself not to overreact, I said, "Everyone loves delicious food."

Brock joined us. "You and Rhonda are in for a few surprises. Right, Jonny?"

Jonny studied me with narrowed eyes and nodded, sending a shiver down my spine.

CHAPTER EIGHT

AFTER THE DINNER GUESTS LEFT, I MADE SURE THE STAFF was cleaning up the private dining room and then went to see Rhonda.

She was sitting at a table outside the kitchen in fine spirits talking with Chet.

When she saw me, she said, "I was just telling Chet that when we first started the hotel this is what it was like—me cooking and you entertaining. It feels good, but, Annie, I'm exhausted."

I laughed. "The two of you did a fabulous job with the meal. As you saw, the Ambassador loved it."

"Jonny didn't like it at all," said Rhonda. "I say screw him. We have our own business to run."

"Do you know Philippa?" I asked Chet. "It looked like you recognized one another."

"I met her at a friend's party in New York City. She and I spent some time together that night and then she disappeared. After realizing who she was and what her family is like, I get it. We're not a match."

Seeing Chet's discomfort, I dropped the subject. "After the dinner, Jonny spoke to the group telling them he wanted Enrico's support for his new restaurant. Enrico quickly shut him down, saying it was no time for business. I quickly thanked people for coming, ending their silent standoff. It was uncomfortable. Jonny left unhappy with me, the evening, seeing Chet, everything."

"I tried to tell Rhonda I shouldn't go into the dining room," said Chet.

Rhonda held up her hand to stop him. "We're not hiding you," she said to Chet. "No matter how hard they try to pull us into their game, we have to stay strong. We can't ruin our reputations or that of the hotel."

"Agreed," I said, recalling the venom coming from Jonny. Brock was Brock and didn't scare me. He was just very annoying.

"I'm calling it a night," said Rhonda getting to her feet. She turned to Chet. "Thanks for everything. Please don't leave until you have Jean-Luc's permission."

"I'll walk you out," I said. "Housekeeping is scheduled to come in to take care of the private dining room after it's cleared of food and dishes."

We left the hotel together, exiting through the back of the hotel to where we'd parked.

Heading toward my car, I stopped and stared in disbelief. "Oh, my God! Look!"

Two of my tires were flat. Even from a short distance, I could tell the tires had been slashed.

"This has to be tied to Jonny Arno's team," said Rhonda. "I can't think of anyone else who'd do something like this." She went over to her car. "My tires are okay."

"I'll call security. Don't wait around for me," I said letting out a tired sigh. "I know how exhausted you are."

"Annie, I won't leave you like this. We're partners, and partners stick together."

We looked up as a member of our hotel security came toward us.

I showed him what had happened.

"We'll check the security cameras and try to find out who did this. It looks like someone came up from the beach." He pointed to the sandy footprints leading to the car.

"The breeze is already blowing them away," I said.

"Why don't I arrange for someone to drive you home?" the guard said.

"I can do that," said Rhonda.

"Okay. We'll take photos and see what we can find," the guard promised.

"Thank you. I'll go with Rhonda and leave you to your work," I said, looking around nervously. I felt violated. It was scary knowing some deranged person was this angry at me.

I climbed into the car with Rhonda, and she turned to me. "I'm sorry, Annie. I know you're upset. So am I. But let's keep this quiet. We'll do some investigation on our own."

"I don't think Brock did it. Do you?"

Rhonda harrumphed. "I can't imagine him getting his hands dirty like this. But he might have arranged it. He's more the sleezy behind-the-scenes kind of guy."

"Maybe we should ask Chet to leave," I said, then shook my head. "No, forget that. We can't let people like Jonny or Brock intimidate us. We were here first."

"You got that right," said Rhonda. "We're not going to let these bastards scare us."

She drove up to my house and stopped the car. "Do you need a ride tomorrow?"

"No, thanks. I'll take one of Vaughn's cars," I said. "Thanks for dropping me off."

"Anytime. I'll be in late tomorrow morning. I'm going to a teacher's meeting with Angie. Evan is doing so well in school that they're thinking of moving him up to 8th grade. I told her that might be a mistake, but I'll support her decision. We'll see."

"Each child is so different," I said. "How's Sally Kate doing?"

"Better, now that she knows she's not stupid. Funny, she's

so eager to work hard to make the situation better. Evan, on the other hand, is lazy because schoolwork comes easily to him."

"They're adorable children. I'm so glad we get to live and work by our children and grandchildren." I frowned at the sudden thought. "You don't think Jonny will try to get to our families, do you?"

"No," Rhonda said quickly, but I'd seen a look of horror flash across her face.

I opened the door and got out of the car, wishing we'd never agreed to host a dinner for Ambassador Ferrara.

The next morning, I pulled Vaughn's SUV up to the front of the hotel for valet parking. I didn't think anyone would be slashing tires in that area.

I was climbing the front stairs when a security guard approached me. "Morning, Ms. Sanders. I have a report for you."

"Thank you. Please come to my office."

We walked together through the lobby and to the back of the hotel to my office, where we could have privacy.

I ushered the guard, a man who'd worked for us for years, inside and indicated for him to take a seat by my desk.

Still upset by the memory of last night's episode, I sat behind my desk and faced him. "What did you find out?"

"The cameras caught the figure of a man slashing the tires. Unfortunately, he was wearing a mask and non-distinguishable clothing. Though we saw evidence of sandy footprints, nothing could be traced because onshore breezes prevented them from remaining in a pattern. We can say the person whom we suspect is male and is of average height and weight."

"In other words, we have nothing to identify the person," I said, sighing.

"I'm sorry," the guard said. "We'll be patrolling that area more frequently."

"Yes, I think you should. Jonny Arno with the new Osteria Arno restaurant up the beach is not happy with us, and I'd hate to see any bad behavior escalate. Both Rhonda and I think he and his people had something to do with this."

"I see," said the guard. "I'll make a note of it on the report."

After the guard left, I went into the kitchen to say hello to Consuela and grab a cup of coffee and a sweet roll. I needed both.

Consuela turned when I approached her. "Hi, Annie. I heard about your car. When Manny saw it out back with the tires slashed, he was upset. Are you okay?"

"I'm fine, but I worry this might be one in a string of retaliations for hiring Chet. I know it sounds crazy, but it happens."

"Chet is a fine young man," said Consuela firmly. "You and Rhonda should be able to hire anyone you want."

"I know," I said. "I hate conflict of any kind." I felt the sting of tears.

She gave me a quick hug. "It'll be all right, Ann." She plated a sweet roll and handed it to me. "Sit. Have some coffee and something to eat. Things will seem better then."

"Just talking to you makes me feel better," I said, meaning it.

As I was sitting at the kitchen table outside the cooking area, Chet arrived.

" 'Morning. I'm glad to see you here so early," I said.

Chet bobbed his head at me. "I said I'd work the early shift to help prepare for the Ambassador's luncheon, then take a break before the wedding dinner tonight. Jean-Luc said that will be a true test of my skill. Wedding dinner and a busy Saturday night at the hotel."

"I'm happy you and Jean-Luc are getting along," I said. "It's a win-win for both of you."

Chet gave me a long look. "Thank you. That means a lot to me. I noticed Jonny's expression when he saw me at dinner last night. He's not happy with either of us."

"Rhonda and I can't let someone like that try to derail our business over petty jealousy," I said firmly. I decided not to tell him about the tires on my car. I didn't want to start his day with bad news, though he'd probably find out about it on his own."

I put my empty plate in the sink and took my coffee to my office. It was going to be a long day.

Later, as I was going over financial papers for the wedding, I thought about how important weddings were to our business. Not only did they usually put 'heads in beds', but they produced a lot of income through meals and special events like afternoon teas or spa treatments.

I called Lorraine to see how this wedding was going and was surprised to have Annette answer the call. "Hi, Annette! What's up? Where's Lorraine?"

"She's at the hospital with Arthur. He wasn't feeling well, and she was worried he was having a stroke."

"Oh, my! That sounds like more than a worry. Is there anything I can do to help?"

"Actually, there is. A breakfast buffet is laid out for the wedding guests in the library. Would you mind going there to greet the guests? I have to stay in the office to take care of some things for the ceremony, which is at four o'clock."

"Not a problem. Anything else?"

"Would you make sure the flowers from the rehearsal dinner last night are on the buffet table?"

"Of course. Please let me know if you get any news about Arthur. Thanks."

I left the office and went to the library, which was now a very versatile event room for us. This morning it was set up for a buffet with round tables spread comfortably throughout the space and would remain a hospitality room for wedding guests until tomorrow.

I noticed the floral centerpiece and saw a plentiful array of stainless steel serving pieces keeping a variety of dishes warm.

Standing, assessing the room, I heard someone came up beside me. I turned and smiled at the mother-of-the-bride who had already proven to be difficult.

"Hello," I said cheerfully. "Beautiful day for a wedding."

"Breezy for a beach wedding, but we'll have to deal with it. And this breakfast buffet was a little late in getting set up," the woman said with a sniff of disapproval.

"We're lucky it isn't a rainy day. Weather at this time of year can be iffy with hurricane season about to start in earnest. And there was a health emergency for Lorraine Grace," I said. "But I promise you that you and your wedding party will be well taken care of."

"I should think so, after all the money we're spending," said the woman.

I held back a groan. No wonder Lorraine and Annette had complained about her.

A few guests wandered into the room, and I stood by so the mother-of-the-bride could welcome them. They seemed like a friendly group, more easygoing than the woman I'd just been talking to. I left the library and headed back to my office.

When I arrived at my office, Lindsay was waiting for me. Her blue eyes shone with happiness when I greeted her with a hug. Lindsay was going to meet Catarina and Philippa to show them around.

We'd first met Amelia Swanson when she called to ask Rhonda and me to hide her sister, Lindsay, at the hotel. She was escaping an abusive husband, the brother of the president. It wasn't our first introduction to messy political situations, but it was the worst for many reasons, especially because of Lindsay's injuries.

While she was staying at the hotel, Lindsay met Jean-Luc and they discovered they liked talking to one another. Those conversations with Jean-Luc, who was recovering from his wife's death, helped them both. For Jean-Luc, it was a second chance at love. For Lindsay, it meant learning to trust a man could be as kind and loving as he was. Now, they were happily married and the parents of two children.

"Thank you for giving Catarina and Philippa a tour of the town," I said. "I'm sure Amelia told you how anxious they are to find a place in Florida they can retire to, if even on a part-time basis."

"Oh, yes. My sister gave me strict instructions on what to do," Lindsay said with a knowing look. "She's always the older sister making sure everything is the way she wants it to be. I love her, though. She saved my life."

"And how are the boys?" I asked her.

"Great. They're a handful, but I'm blessed to have them. And Jean-Luc is crazy about them." A doting father, Jean-Luc was in his fifties when their sons were born. Jacques, the oldest at five, followed by Damon.

I asked, "Are you still working at the Women's Shelter?"

"Oh, yes," said Lindsay. "One afternoon a week I act as receptionist, and I'm available anytime to respond to emergency calls. I was lucky to escape my situation. I don't ever forget it. Especially the way you and Rhonda took me in."

We hugged, and then I checked my watch. "We'd better head to the lobby. We're to meet Catarina and Philippa there."

Lindsay was quiet as we walked to the lobby.

"Thank you again for doing this," I said. "After you give them a tour, please come back to the hotel. Jean-Luc is preparing a special lunch for the family and a small group of businesspeople in town and I know he'll want you there." I'd been relieved to note that neither Jonny Arno nor Brock Goodwin's name was on the guest list.

Catarina and Philippa were sitting on a couch in the lobby when we approached them. Catarina got to her feet, turned, and motioned for Philippa to rise.

Lindsay and I faced them together.

"Hello," I said. "Meet your tour guide, Lindsay Rodin. Lindsay, this is Catarina and Philippa Ferrara. I know you'll have a pleasant morning. Then, luncheon will be served at one o'clock here at the hotel. Jean-Luc, Lindsay's husband, is preparing a special meal for you."

"It all sounds delightful," Catarina said politely, and the smile she gave Lindsay was genuinely warm.

Satisfied that the three of them would get along, I left to go check on Lorraine.

When I walked into the office, Annette was on the phone. She ended the call and gave me a thumbs-up signal. "That was Lorraine. Good news! They're still doing tests on Arthur, but so far nothing indicates a stroke. He was disoriented for a moment, but they think it's attributable to what they're calling the flu. They've tested for Covid. But it's not that."

"I'm so glad it's nothing worse," I said.

"Me, too," said Annette. "Lorraine will be here this afternoon before the wedding, but she won't stay through the dinner afterwards. No worries. Lauren and I and the rest of the staff will take care of it."

"Thanks so much, Annette," I said. "I don't know what we'd do without you."

A smile spread across Annette's face. "I'm glad to be here. It's wonderful that I'm able to work at the same hotel as Bernie."

"Well, you're much more than staff. You're family," I said, meaning it. Our hotel had brought people together and formed a family of its own.

When I got back to the office, Rhonda was sitting there, looking at her computer screen and frowning.

"Hi. What's up?" I asked her.

"Sorry to be gone so long," Rhonda said. "Angie and I met with Evan's teacher and then went for a tour at the private academy in town that the teacher recommended to Angie and Reggie."

"How did you like it?" I asked.

"I was impressed," Rhonda admitted. "But I want him to have a rounded school experience. Fun, too."

"What does Angie think?" I asked.

"She thought it was great, a better fit for Evan. I told her I'd pay for it," said Rhonda. "If it's what will help Evan, I'm all for it."

"I'm glad you're making this decision so early in the school year," I said.

"Yes, that's why his teacher didn't want to let more time go by. It's early enough that Evan should fit right in. What's going on here?"

I told Rhonda all that had happened. "Everything's under control, but it does make me wonder why some weddings are so difficult."

"A lot depends on the bride and her mother," said Rhonda.

"Yes," I agreed, looking up as someone knocked on the door.

"Come in," Rhonda called.

Bernie walked into the office and closed the door behind him. "Ann! I heard what happened to your car last night. I wanted to check with you to see how you're dealing with it."

"Honestly, I've been so busy this morning I haven't had much time for it to sink in. But last night, I admit I was scared by the idea that we all might be targeted by someone who'd stoop that low. I'm not saying it's Jonny Arno and his team who are responsible, but I can't help thinking they're connected somehow."

"Me too," said Bernie, giving us a worried look. "It was a petty thing to do, and we don't want this to escalate in any way. Yet, we can't and shouldn't be prevented from carrying on our business as we see fit."

"That bastard needs to be watched carefully," said Rhonda.

"I've already spoken to our security team about the situation," Bernie said. "More than patrolling the area, I've arranged for a guard to appear incognito in the hotel bar this evening. We'll tell the bartenders to be aware of what's happening, so if they see anyone that they think is suspicious or if they overhear any antagonistic talk about the hotel, they can alert the guard."

"Smart thinking, Bernie," said Rhonda.

"The kitchen area will be watched," said Bernie. "How did Chet do at his job?"

"Very well," I answered. "He's doing a double shift today to help with the wedding while Jean-Luc is preparing the luncheon. I admire his flexibility and willingness to work."

"Excellent," said Bernie. "I don't want anyone getting hurt because we're making a stand against others telling us what to do."

"I agree," I said. "But the look of venom Jonny gave me last night was frightening. What kind of man does that?"

"An egotistical man who knows he's failing," said Bernie. "I talked to a few friends in Miami, and they say that Jonny left Chez Michel not out of choice but because they were losing business."

"He's trying to blame us for his problems," said Rhonda. "Let's keep an eye on Brock who's only too willing to help Jonny out."

"Agreed." Bernie's normally stern face softened. "I don't want you or anyone else to get hurt."

"I wonder who's behind Jonny in all this. There have to be other people helping him with a new restaurant," I said.

"It could be anyone," said Bernie. "Not all of them bad. For now, let's take it one day at a time."

"Right. We've got a wedding to get through. Annette has been a wonderful help with this group," I said.

"She's pleasant with people," said Bernie, a note of pride in his voice.

Rhonda and I exchanged a look of amusement. She'd taken stiff, proper Bernie and turned him into a marshmallow who adored his wife.

CHAPTER NINE

AFTER BERNIE LEFT, I SAID TO RHONDA, "LET'S TAKE A break on the beach. I want to talk about Lorraine and Arthur. Lorraine needs more and more time away from the hotel to be with him. While it's understandable, and I don't have any problem with her doing so, it leaves the hotel needing more help."

"I agree. I'm glad they got married when they did because Arthur's health is beginning to fail," said Rhonda. "Angie told me she and Reggie are concerned."

We left the office and headed to the beach. Even though it was a bit windy, it felt freeing to be out in fresh air.

I kicked off my sandals and headed right to the water's lacy edge. There was something about standing in the water, admiring the birds above me and those little ones skittering along the sand that anchored me. The scene gave me a moment to breathe and to let go of the tension in my shoulders.

Rhonda stood on the sand behind me looking back at the hotel.

I turned around and took it in.

The two-story, pink stucco building reminded me of a lazy Roseate Spoonbill nestled on the sand enjoying the sun. In truth, it was a stunning hotel offering an array of services to pampered guests. Rhonda and I often referred to it as our baby, and we shared a mother's pride when we looked at what we'd created.

"What did you want to talk about regarding Lorraine?"

asked Rhonda. "I think we need to give Annette a raise and the title of Wedding Planner to match Lorraine. Then we should move Lauren from assistant to Lorraine to Wedding Planning Office Manager. It gives both Annette and Lauren a little more authority without taking away anything from Lorraine."

"Wow! You have been thinking of this for a while," said Rhonda. "It sounds okay to me. But we still need to keep Annette as Special Events Coordinator."

"I agree. It's just with Lorraine gone, I'd like to be able to introduce Annette as one of our wedding planners."

Rhonda gave me a thoughtful nod. "You're right. It'll make our wedding guests happy to be able to deal directly with a wedding planner, whether it's Lorraine or Annette."

I heard my name being called and turned to see Brock walking toward us.

"Oh, that bastard. Let's hurry back to the hotel," said Rhonda. "He's nothing but bad news."

"I want to hear what he obviously wants to tell us. Look at him waving his hand to us."

"I wonder if he's heard about your car tires," Rhonda said.

"There's no way for him to know anything about it. If he mentions it, we know he had something to do with it," I said, growing angry as I talked.

I forced myself to remain calm as Brock walked up to us with a swagger I'd come to detest.

"Hello, ladies," he said. "How are things going with your new chef? I heard he wants to come back and work for Jonny."

"I don't know where you heard such a thing. He's happy at The Beach House Hotel," I said. "How's the new restaurant coming along? When will the renovations be done?"

"Not for a couple more weeks," said Brock. "It's going to be beautiful. A real showcase." He cocked an eyebrow. "I heard you had a little trouble at the hotel last night."

I frowned and shook my head. "Not that I know of. What are you talking about?"

"Oh, nothing. Just a rumor, I guess. A lot of them are floating around about how people are tired of The Beach House Hotel and can't wait for Osteria Arno to open. Guess you'll be working hard to try and compete."

"That's bullshit and you know it, Brock. Our guests love us just the way we are," said Rhonda.

"We'll see. Want to put money on it?" sneered Brock.

"Sure," said Rhonda. "How much?"

"A couple thousand?" taunted Brock.

I kept quiet. A couple of thousand wasn't much to Rhonda but it could mean quite a bit to Brock who was always struggling to keep up the image of a wealthy man. It worried me he was so confident.

Rhonda held out her hand. "Okay, five thousand dollars that your restaurant won't ruin the business at our dining room."

"Oh, well, I didn't mean to make such a big wager. Let's not go there," said Brock, backpedaling as fast as he could. He liked people to think he had a lot of money, but we knew he didn't. "Let's just see what happens. The proof is in the pudding, as they say. Okay, I'd better go. I'm helping to furnish the restaurant with items from my import business."

As he trotted away, I turned to Rhonda with a triumphant grin. "That's how Brock was able to go into business with Jonny Arno's group. I bet he's not charging them for decorative items in exchange for a very small part of the business."

"It makes me wonder how Jonny is financing the rest of it," said Rhonda. "On our way back to the office, let's check in with Chet. I want to know if he's unhappy working with us. I don't want any second thoughts about hiring him."

"Fair enough," I said. "I can tell you he's been busy all morning and is even willing to split shifts because of the wedding."

"We also need to see how Harper did at the bar last night. I hear it was mobbed with wedding guests and weekend warriors," said Rhonda. She checked her watch. "Harper's not due in for a while."

"I think she might be serving drinks at the luncheon today," I said. "Let's find out."

We went inside the hotel and right to the kitchen. Breakfast was over, and lunch was being prepared along with some items for the wedding dinner and regular offerings on the dinner menu.

We caught Chet's eye and motioned for him to come talk to us standing at the door.

He trotted over. "Hi. What's up?"

Rhonda gave him a stern look. "We heard from someone associated with Osteria Arno that you want to go work for them when they open. Is that true?"

"What? No. Absolutely not. Who told you that?" he said, clearly upset. "This might have to do with a phone call I received last night. A man called and told me he was speaking for Jonny. That Jonny was sorry he fired me and wants me back to cook for him. I told him to eff off."

I shot Rhonda a worried look. "I don't like the sound of this."

"Did he say anything more?" Rhonda asked Chet.

"Yeah. He told me I'd be sorry," said Chet. "I figure it's Jonny being a bully again."

"We have an empty staff apartment here at the hotel over

the garage and spa," I said. "Why don't you move in there until things calm down?"

"Great idea," said Rhonda. "Where are you staying now?"

Chet gave an embarrassed shrug. "At a cheap motel outside of town. Harper and I are sharing the cost."

"During your break today why don't you check out? We'll get housekeeping to prepare the apartment for you. And Harper, if that's what you two want to do," I said.

Chet held up a hand. "We're just friends. But, yeah, it would help her too. Thanks."

"We just don't want anything to happen to you," said Rhonda. "You've been totally open with us. We want you working here."

"I want that, too," said Chet. "I'm already learning a lot from Jean-Luc, who's nothing like Jonny. Thanks. I've got to get back to work."

Chet left us and I turned to Rhonda. "I really like him. Let's hope we can keep him safe here at the hotel. The thought of him being vulnerable in a motel is pretty frightening."

"I agree," said Rhonda. "Jonny Arno is not a nice man and doesn't want anyone else to succeed. Let's tell Bernie and security what we're doing with the apartment."

By the time we held a short meeting with them, it was time for Harper to show up to help with the luncheon.

Rhonda and I checked the private dining room. A total of twenty-four people were invited for lunch with Enrico, including Bernie and a couple of other people in hospitality and several members of the business community in the area.

When Harper walked across the lobby wearing her uniform of a black skirt and white blouse, she saw us and waved.

"Thank you," she said as she approached. "I got a call from Chet. He told me we have a place to stay right here on the hotel property. That's so gracious of you."

"We think it'll be safer for you," I said.

Harper grimaced. "I understand Jonny's people are threatening Chet. A friend of mine who still lives in Miami said she's heard that the owners of Chez Michel are trying to make Jonny pay for not keeping his part of the contract agreement to increase sales. He must be desperate to succeed here on this coast."

"How did last night go at the bar?" Rhonda asked.

"Great. The wedding crowd is a bunch of drinkers. And several others came in, including young people who'd seen your new ad for canapes at the hotel. A few of them mentioned they were friends of Angie and Liz. I kept watch on what they were drinking and eating. I agree that we can do better with that age group. There's definitely a place for them here."

"I hope you're making careful notes for Angie and Liz so you can come up with plans the three of you agree on," I said.

"Oh, yes," said Harper. "Sorry, I have to go meet Annette."

We followed her into the private dining room. Instead of a long table like last night, four round tables for six were spread across the area. A small bar was set up in the back corner and a dais held a lectern and a microphone.

Each table held a small centerpiece with the same Italian flag color theme as last night.

Annette walked into the room behind us. "I think we're ready. The four waitresses are coming, and I see Harper is here."

"Thanks, Annette. How is the wedding dinner shaping up?"

"Fine. Lauren and Lorraine are handling that." She greeted four waitresses who arrived with a cart holding iced water pitchers. "Okay, we have four minutes until our guests arrive. Please pour the water in the goblets and remove the cart."

Not wanting to be in their way, Rhonda and I left.

Outside the door, we saw Caterina and Philippa standing

with Lindsay.

"How did the tour go?" I asked.

"Very well. I've fallen in love with Sabal and realize I'm going to need a lot more time than I thought to consider where we might want to live. I'm meeting with the Luna brothers tomorrow, but that won't be nearly enough time. Do you think we could rent one of the guesthouses for a week or so?"

"Let me check the reservations schedule and see what we can do," said Rhonda. "After the luncheon, come see us in our office. We'll make arrangements of some kind that will please you."

"Yes, we'll do our best," I said.

Enrico came over to us. "Thank you for setting up everything for our meeting today. I'm hoping it will be beneficial to all in the community."

"I'm curious. Is Jonny Arno one of the invited guests today?" I asked him.

"No." He grimaced. "He called me this morning. He claims we're distant cousins." Enrico shook his head. "It could be possible. In Sicily, many families are intertwined and go back generations. I'll follow up."

"We'll do our best to put Catarina and Philippa in one of the guesthouses," I said.

"Thank you. It's easy to see why Amelia Swanson recommended Sabal and your hotel," he said. He turned away to greet one of the guests heading toward the private dining room.

Rhonda and I went back to our office to check the reservations schedule.

"We can move the one couple who was supposed to stay there for one night to the Presidential Suite. That will give Catarina and Enrico the guesthouse for eight straight days," I said. "More, if necessary."

"Okay. That's better planning. I see that the reservation for the couple was not guaranteed. That makes it easy," said Rhonda.

"They'll be thrilled with a stay in the Presidential Suite," I said. "A win-win for all."

"I want to check on the employee apartment for Chet and Harper," Rhonda said. "I wish we were able to build more than the three apartments we have."

"With the expansion of the laundry room and spa, there wasn't room," I said.

Rhonda and I left our office and went over to the building which at one time was simply a six-car garage. It had changed considerably over the years and now, with additions, housed the spa, laundry room, and three staff apartments. All had beautiful views over gardens and the two tennis courts we had installed for both tennis and pickleball.

Each apartment had two bedrooms, two bathrooms, a living/dining room, small laundry area, and a decent-sized kitchen with a small eating area. The largest one was occupied by Consuela and Manny. The other two were used by a variety of staffers on a short-term basis. Now, one of the other apartments was temporarily housing a young couple with a baby who were waiting to purchase a house of their own. He was working for Manny on the landscaping crew, and she was employed in the housekeeping department. This flexibility allowed us to find long-term employees, which was so important in the hospitality industry where employee turnover was a problem.

We knocked and walked into the apartment to be used by Chet and Harper. The housekeeping staff had done a great job of getting it ready. A vase of fresh flowers sat on the coffee table in the living room, and bottles of cold water sat in the refrigerator, along with a platter of cheese, fruit, and crackers.

We checked the bedrooms. It appeared that Harper's things were in one bedroom and Chet's in the other.

"Guess they really are just friends," said Rhonda. "It's none of my business, but I'm glad they're not dating. Any break-up might affect us, and I must confess until things get settled with Jonny Arno, I don't want anything else to worry about."

"I agree," I said, feeling a shiver crawl down my back even as we stepped outside into bright, warm sunlight.

"Guess, we'd better get ready for the wedding," Rhonda said. "I'll meet you back at the hotel in a few minutes. I'm going home to change clothes and to check on the kids."

"Me, too," I said. "It might be wise for us to be around. Harper said it's a drinking crowd, and you never know what that might mean."

"Sometimes it feels as if we're babysitters," grumbled Rhonda, and I couldn't blame her. Though our guests were very different, we felt a responsibility for all of them.

When I arrived back at the hotel later that evening, I was pleased to see a security guard patrolling the area. I got out of my car, waved to him, and entered the hotel anxious to see if everything was prepared for the wedding ceremony. Though the ceremony itself was going to be on the beach, there was much to prepare both in the hotel and outside.

Guests were asked to gather in the library and then to make their way to the beach where a wooden arch decorated with flowers was in place, along with a small lectern for the minister presiding over the ceremony.

The bride had chosen fall colors for her wedding. While guests were lining up and preparing to walk to the beach, the three bridesmaids showed up wearing coral silk tea-length slip dresses. They looked adorable—so young, so eager. At their innocence, my eyes smarted with the sting of tears.

I met Rhonda outside by the boardwalk, and we stood together as guests walked by. In the background, a guitar player was playing soft classical music. He suddenly changed music and the parents of the groom, the mother of the bride, and the first of the bridesmaids walked by us.

The music changed once more, and the bride appeared on the boardwalk with her father. A pretty girl with red hair, she wore a simple white silk sleeveless dress that hung just above her ankles. On her head she wore a collection of flowers tucked into the French knot at the back of her head. The effect was stunning.

I glanced at Rhonda.

As usual, she was dabbing at tears she couldn't contain. It was always this way. We'd seen many weddings and would continue to do so, but each one was special in its own way. Even though the mother of this bride had been difficult, the bride herself was a sweet young woman who was marrying the man she'd helped through medical school.

Once the bride had passed by, Rhonda and I hurried behind the sunset deck and building to watch the ceremony. The groom and the rest of his party were wearing tan slacks and coral golf shirts. The smile on his face as he gazed at his bride walking toward him brought fresh tears to Rhonda and had me dabbing at my own eyes.

At the end of the ceremony, as the guests were applauding, Rhonda and I slipped away to make sure the reception was ready to receive guests.

We checked the dining room. Both Lorraine and Annette were talking in the area reserved for the wedding party.

"Cocktails and canapés are being served on the pool deck,"

said Lorraine. "The dinner is well-organized here."

"Thanks so much. It all looks fantastic," I said.

Lorraine cleared her throat. "Heads up. The mother of the bride, who's been so difficult to work with, had a lot of champagne this afternoon. We'll keep an eye on her, but it could mean trouble."

"If there's anything you need, let us know," said Rhonda. "Annie and I are going to check on guests who've moved to one of the guesthouses, and then I'm going home."

Lorraine gave us a little salute, and we walked away.

We took the private walkway to the two guesthouses on the property. These accommodations were important for guests who especially needed privacy for a number of days. It would be the perfect place for Catarina and Philippa to hide out.

"I'm glad we could juggle things around so that the Ambassador's family could stay here," I said as we approached the guesthouse reserved for them. "I can't shake the idea that Jonny is going to continue to be a problem. And with little enthusiasm from the Ambassador for his new restaurant, Jonny could try something stupid with his family."

"Oh, my God! I didn't think of that, Annie. Would he be that stupid?" said Rhonda.

"He's allowing Brock Goodwin to be part of his team. That says a lot about how smart he is."

"You're right. Before I leave the hotel, I'll speak to the security team and Bernie. I'll feel better if I do," said Rhonda.

"Thanks. I'm going home and taking a swim in the pool to relax," I said, wanting to shake off the bad feelings I couldn't get rid of after seeing the slashed tires on my car.

We rang the bell of the guesthouse and waited for an answer.

Philippa came to the door wearing a bikini that showed off her young, taut body to perfection. "Hello. Please come in. My parents and I want to thank you for finding this accommodation for us."

As we stepped inside, Catarina walked toward us wearing a coverup. "Thank you, Ann and Rhonda, for allowing us to stay in this lovely house. Enrico had to go back to New York City, but my daughter and I will stay here for as long as it takes to find a place to live."

"We're glad we could do this for you," said Rhonda. "If you need anything, just call the front desk."

"I saw a wedding going on at the beach," said Philippa. "How romantic. I'm sure you have plenty of beach weddings here. It's so lovely."

"Yes, we do," said Rhonda. "Each one is very special."

"We won't keep you," I said. "We just wanted to make sure you were comfortably settled."

"Thank you again," said Catarina, shaking our hands.

Rhonda and I left, and I quickly gathered my things from the office and went home, exhausted.

CHAPTER TEN

I FROWNED AS I PULLED INTO THE DRIVEWAY. LIANA'S car wasn't there.

I parked in the garage and went to the kitchen door. I opened it and waited for Cindy to greet me.

When she didn't appear, I knew something was very wrong... or very right!

I hurried onto the lanai and looked down at the dock. Vaughn and Robbie were there sitting on the sailboat talking, Cindy curled in Vaughn's lap.

My heart pounding with anticipation, I dropped my purse and ran down the grassy slope to greet them.

Vaughn stepped onto the dock and wrapped his arms around me. "Thought I'd surprise you. We got through earlier than I thought."

"It couldn't come at a better time," I said, lifting my face for his kiss.

"I've waited for this," said Vaughn, lowering his lips to mine.

While we kissed, Cindy pranced at our feet and Robbie let out a small grunt.

Laughing, I pulled away from Vaughn. "Guess we'll have more privacy later. But I'm so glad you're home. Talking on the phone just isn't the same as having you with me."

"I sensed something has been bothering you and figured you'd tell me when you were ready," said Vaughn, cupping my cheeks in his hands and giving me a steady look of concern.

"You're right, but for the moment, I just want to enjoy

being with you. Are we going for a sail?"

"It's a nice evening for one with a steady, manageable breeze. Are you up for it?" Wearing a T-shirt and shorts, he looked ... well, yummy.

"I'm definitely ready for some time with my family. I need to let the fresh air take away some of my stress. Just give me time to change."

"Great." Vaughn gave me another kiss. "Robbie and I have already put together a picnic for us for supper. Simple stuff."

"That sounds perfect," I said, and eagerly went into the house.

As I was changing clothes, my body felt as if a huge weight had been lifted from me. I didn't want Vaughn to know how threatened I'd felt by Jonny's unreasonable reaction to our hiring Chet. But as Bernie, Rhonda, and I had agreed, we couldn't allow Jonny to interfere with our business. But a part of me knew Vaughn would be upset that once more Amelia's connection to our guests was bringing us trouble.

When I returned to the dock in jeans and a long-sleeved knit shirt, Vaughn and Robbie were ready to take off.

Sailing had been a way for Vaughn and Robbie to bond in their early years together. Robbie had been only a toddler hanging onto the wheel of the boat with Vaughn when we first started sailing with him. Now, Vaughn was sitting in the cockpit watching as Robbie skillfully steered the boat away from the dock.

We motored through the inlet, passed condos built along the water's edge and out to the open Gulf.

While Vaughn and Robbie raised sails, I held onto the wheel and then turned it over to Robbie who steered the boat to fall off the wind and allow the sails to fill on a close reach.

Skimming silently across the water, I breathed in the fresh air and leaned back against a cushion in the cockpit. This moment was a blessing I vowed never to forget. My family enjoying time together with nature is what made the work Vaughn and I did worth it. We were so very lucky.

Vaughn moved over to sit beside me. He placed his arm around me and pulled me close. "I love you, you know," he said softly into my ear.

I turned to him with a smile. "Me, too. You."

We chuckled together.

"Okay, we're going to come about," said Robbie.

Vaughn held onto the mainsheet and allowed the sail to swing across the cockpit as the boat tacked to a different heading.

Moving in the opposite direction, we settled down to some smooth, easy sailing. With the threat of storms and hurricanes, fall could be a tricky time weatherwise. But tonight was perfect for us.

Later, we anchored the boat so we could all enjoy the picnic Vaughn and Robbie had put together.

Sitting with two of my favorite people in the cockpit, gently rocking with the waves that caressed our boat, I felt blessed beyond words.

Vaughn seemed to understand and put his arm around me. "Nice, huh?"

I smiled at him and turned to Robbie.

"You're getting to be such a competent sailor," I said. "I remember the first time we took you out on a boat. You were just a toddler but even then, you loved being on the water."

"It's a fun time," said Robbie.

"Yes, we all miss Dad when he's away working," I said. "I'm thinking it's time to get the Ts interested in learning to sail. Gabe is too young, but maybe we can work as a team to make it happen with his older siblings."

"Short trips to begin with," said Vaughn. "And it has to be balanced —the three of us and the three of them. Too many things can go wrong if we're not careful. And the Ts can be trouble.

I laughed. "They are the best thing to happen to us all. They've brought our family even closer. And now little Gabe is here to keep Noah company dealing with his sisters."

"I'm not going to get married for a long time," said Robbie.

"You have years ahead of you before that should happen," said Vaughn. "But when it's with the right woman, you'll know. And then you won't want to wait."

Vaughn was still mourning the death of his first wife when we met. But early on, we both knew we had something special, worth pursuing.

We finished eating, and while I packed up, Robbie and Vaughn prepared the boat to return to our dock.

Back at the house, Cindy greeted us with looks of reproach. We'd decided not to take her on this short sail, and she still was unhappy about it.

I picked her up and hugged her. "Next time, Cindy."

She kissed my cheek and wiggled to get down to go over to Robbie for equal treatment.

Watching the two of them together, I knew we'd made the right decision to get another Dachshund, after Trudy died.

We got the food sorted out and dishes in the dishwasher, then the three of us looked at one another.

"I'm going to watch television," said Robbie. "Night. Thanks for the sail."

I kissed Robbie and said to Vaughn, "I'm going to bed. It's been a hectic week."

"I'm right behind you," said Vaughn.

I quickly got ready for bed and had just placed my head on my pillow when Vaughn joined me.

He pulled me close. "I've missed you," he whispered in my ear, sending a tingling of expectation throughout my body.

I rolled over and faced him. "It's never the same with you gone. I'm so glad you're home."

"Not as happy as I am," he said. He caressed my face and moved his hands lower.

My fatigue evaporated as we began to show one another just how special our marriage was.

Later, while Vaughn slept, I lay awake hoping Vaughn wouldn't hear about Rhonda's and my troubles with Jonny Arno. Vaughn normally didn't interfere in my business, but he would be upset to know that anything amiss was going on.

CHAPTER ELEVEN

I AWOKE EARLY, REFRESHED AND HAPPY. BESIDE ME Vaughn was snoring softly. Pleased I didn't have any hotel duties today, I slipped out of bed and drew on a pair of shorts and a T-shirt to go for a walk on the beach. It was my favorite way to start a day.

After letting Cindy outside, I went to the garage and climbed into my car.

The sun was rising, sending rosy fingers of light into the soft-gray sky. The slight chill in the air was invigorating, especially because it promised to be a hot day.

I parked my car behind the hotel, checking to see if a security guard was nearby. I waved to one and headed out to the beach. Stepping onto the cool surface, I sprinted toward the water's edge. The hard-packed sand nearby was an easier place to walk, but I chose to stand a moment breathing in the salty air, studying the waves rolling into shore and retreating in a soothing pattern.

Sand pipers and sanderlings hurried along the frothy edge of the water, their footprints stamping proof of their existence into the sand.

In the distance I saw two figures, and recognizing them, I went to greet Chet and Phillipa.

Intrigued, I wondered about the one date they'd had in New York City. Or was it more than that?

"Hello," I said, approaching them.

Chet and Philippa faced me, holding hands.

"It's nice to see you here. It's a perfect time of day to be on the beach," I said.

"It's so beautiful", said Philippa. "I really didn't want to come to Florida with my parents." She smiled at Chet. "But if I hadn't come, we wouldn't have had the chance to reconnect. I never thought I'd see Chet again. I lost his information and then he moved ..." Philippa's voice trailed off but the look she gave Chet made me realize this was more than a casual meeting. I wondered what her parents would think.

As if she'd read my thoughts, Philippa said, "Please don't say anything to my mother about this. I need to talk to her myself."

"Oh, yes, of course. We at The Beach House Hotel honor our guests' requests for privacy."

Chet seemed to realize he still held Philippa's hand and let it drop. "I'm on breakfast shift this morning. I'd better go."

He and Philippa gazed at one another.

Out of the corner of my eye, I saw Brock Goodwin trotting toward us.

"Oh, no," I said. "Here comes trouble. Please, just keep any private information to yourselves."

"Morning, ladies and Chet," said Brock. He turned to Chet. "Shouldn't you be working? Or did you decide you owe Jonny a favor?"

"I owe Jonny nothing of the kind," said Chet, drawing himself up, exposing his broad, muscular chest.

Brock backed away. "Someday, you're going to have to deal with him, not me." He faced Philippa. "As president of the Neighborhood Association, I feel it's my duty to make sure that each VIP is welcomed. I'd love to take you to lunch."

Philippa struggled to hide her obvious distaste. "Thank you, but my plans are pretty settled for my entire stay."

"Oh, but ..." Brock began.

I gave him the warning look my kids would recognize.

"We're in the middle of a private conversation, so ..."

"I get it," grumped Brock. "I'm just trying to be neighborly."

Chet shook his head. "See you later," he said to Philippa and me.

After he left, Brock headed off in a different direction.

"Who is that horrible man?" Philippa asked me. "At dinner the other night, he wanted me to have a drink with him. I thought I made it plain I wasn't interested. He's older than my father."

"Brock's ego knows no bounds," I said with disgust. "He's the bane of our existence and would try to do anything to harm Rhonda and me or our hotel."

Philippa shuddered. "I'll stay away from him. I'm going to try to persuade my mother I don't need to look at houses with her today. I'd like a day to simply flop."

"Is she having any luck?" I asked.

"The Luna brothers have promised to show her everything in the entire region. So, I think it's going to take some time. The one thing she knows is that she can't wait to be able to leave New York City and spend time here or at home in Italy."

"Is that why she thinks you should marry someone from home? So you'll be part of her life there?" I asked, aware I was being a bit too inquisitive.

"That's something I need to talk to my mother about," said Philippa. "The idea is about an old family promise. She's caught between wanting to please my father's family and having me close to them and knowing I need my freedom. It all started with an old-fashioned agreement between my grandfather and Luciano Bolino's." She checked her watch. "I'd better go. My mother will be getting up soon."

As I walked back to the hotel, I knew Rhonda would be thrilled with the opportunity to play matchmaker at the hotel.

But I worried about the complications and vowed not to mention it to her.

I went through the back of the hotel to my office to monitor things before going home and spending the day with Vaughn. I checked messages and was surprised to see one from Bernie. It simply said: *Call me.*

I dialed his extension and Bernie answered. "Hello, Ann. You got my message?"

"I did. What's going on?"

"I didn't want to disturb you and Rhonda on your days off, but in case you came in, I wanted to talk to you about an incident last night."

"Oh." My throat tightened with worry.

"The mother of the bride fell outside by the pool last night. She was drunk as a ...what's the word?"

"Skunk? Drunk as a skunk?"

"Yes, that's it. She's claiming she's going to sue the hotel for negligence for not keeping the pool deck dry. This, after several in the wedding party decided to jump into the pool with their clothes on."

"She doesn't have a viable case," I said.

"No," said Bernie. "I have statements from several of the guests regarding the situation and wanted you to be aware if she tries to get in touch with you or Rhonda as she promised she would."

"Thanks for the information," I said. "I'll wait to discuss this with Rhonda. It's been a long week, and we both need a little time off."

"Agreed," said Bernie. "I'm just keeping you in the loop."

"I appreciate that a lot," I said. Bernie was a gem in the business and we were lucky to have him.

###

At home, I placed the warm cinnamon buns I'd brought home from the hotel on the kitchen counter. Then I went to greet Vaughn who was swimming in the pool.

"Morning," I said. "I brought home treats from the hotel."

"Cinnamon rolls?" Vaughn asked, peering into the box with the hotel logo.

"Especially for you from Consuela. I went for a walk on the beach. You were snoring peacefully when I left."

"I figured that's where you were," said Vaughn. "I know how much you like your early morning walks there."

"I'm home for the rest of the day," I said. "What would you like to do?"

"Just relax right here with you," said Vaughn.

"Sounds perfect. I've got a good book, and I intend to do nothing but read for most of the day. I can't remember when I've had a chance to do so,"

"I do want to see Liz and the kids, though," said Vaughn. "They're growing so fast that each time I get to see them, I notice big changes."

"Okay, that sounds like fun. I'll give Liz a call and see if we can invite ourselves over." At one time I'd envisioned having all the kids here at my house for playdates but soon learned visits were handled better at the kids' house, where they had all their toys and could easily be watched.

I went inside and helped myself to a cup of coffee and a sweet roll. Taking them and my cell phone out to the lanai, I settled on the couch to call Liz.

"Hi, Mom! What's up?" she answered cheerfully.

"Vaughn is home, and he wants to see you and the kids. I know it's easier for everyone if we come to your house. Is sometime today workable?"

"Perhaps you could give Chad and me a break and watch them while we go to lunch. Then we'll have time to talk."

"That will be great," I said. "What time do you want us there?"

"How about eleven thirty? That way we can miss most of the touristy crowds," said Liz.

"We can do that. I love that we can give you and Chad a time to yourselves," I said.

"We appreciate it, especially because Chad's mother isn't interested in doing any babysitting. I can't say much to Chad about it because it hurts his feelings that she doesn't ever have time for us."

"That's pretty much how it was for him growing up, wasn't it?"

"Unfortunately, yes," said Liz. "That's why he wants to have an active role in raising the kids. Believe me, it takes more than one person to handle triplets and a toddler."

"Now that Vaughn is home, perhaps the two of you can get away for a sail. As a matter of fact, Vaughn, Robbie, and I were talking about introducing the Ts to sailing. It would be us three adults and the three kids. That's the only way it would work. How does that sound?"

"Excellent," said Liz. "Vaughn is the one that got me into sailing, and it's a delightful way to enjoy nature and to relax. I thought of Dad this morning and realized he never really had time for me growing up."

"Robert loved you, but like you said, he never had time for his family unless it was connected to the business in some way."

"Your business," said Liz. "I know all about how he stole your ideas."

"No use going there," I said. "Look at both of us now, happily married and loving our family times."

"I talked to Chad about carving out time for hotel business and he's all for it," said Liz. "Maybe that's why I'm remembering things."

"One day at a time. Rhonda and I want you and Angie to take over one day. We can talk about it later. Let's set up a meeting with Harper and discuss some of her ideas and yours."

"Thanks, Mom. I needed to hear that today. I realize how fast the kids are growing. When they're all in school all day, I want to have a meaningful life beyond being their mother."

"Understandable," I said. "We'll see you later."

I ended the call and sat a moment thinking how life was one circle after another. I never would've known Rhonda if our daughters hadn't met, and Rhonda would never have met Will if he hadn't been my financial advisor and on and on.

Vaughn approached and leaned down to kiss me. Meeting him was the most magical circle of all.

CHAPTER TWELVE

EACH TIME I SAW MY DARLING GRANDCHILDREN RUN toward me my heart filled with joy. I'd heard from other women how special it was to be a grandparent but hadn't experienced it until my grandchildren were born.

Liz had tried for a baby for a few years before having the triplets. The wait had been worth it. Emily, Olivia, and Noah were bright, active four-year-olds about to become five. Their younger brother, Gabe, who was eighteen months old, had walked early in an effort to keep up with them. Though they played together, each child liked to do their own thing making it difficult to keep an eye on them.

As an only child with no real example to follow, Liz had surprisingly acquired an easy attitude with them, befitting someone from a large family with a lot of experience. It was a pleasure to see.

After bidding Liz and Chad goodbye, Vaughn and I helped the children play in the oversized plastic pool in the backyard. All the kids, even Gabe, had taken swim lessons and though the water in the pool wasn't deep, we watched them carefully. Noah liked playing with the water table, a small table that held a few inches of water in a built-in trough. He liked playing with his cars there, while the girls played house with their plastic dishes and cups in the pool. Gabe was content to sit and splash in the water.

With their parents away, it was interesting to see how the children interacted. For their age, the triplets were pretty nice at sharing and checking up on one another. Gabe followed them around the yard when he could but would sometimes get frustrated and sit and cry.

Both Emily and Olivia were sweet about comforting him, but as the youngest, he couldn't keep up with them.

I lifted Gabe into my arms, not caring that his wet bathing suit was soaking my top. I hugged him, loving the moment. I could see he was getting tired, and while Vaughn watched the other kids, I took Gabe into his room to rock him to sleep. Liz had admitted to me that she and Gabe both liked this special time together. After trying to take care of three at once, Liz was enjoying this little one by herself. I loved having these moments with him, too.

Later, after the Ts were changed out of their bathing suits and given snacks, Vaughn and I sat and read books with them. Vaughn loved playing the parts of characters in the books bringing gales of laughter from the kids.

By the time Liz and Chad returned from lunch and errands, Vaughn, the kids, and I were all tired.

As Vaughn and I left Liz's, he turned to me. "Want to grab a burger at Ken's? I'm really hungry for his special."

"Sounds delicious," I said, realizing we hadn't had lunch, and it was almost suppertime. "Let me check in with Robbie. He and Brett are doing a project together at Brett's house."

I called Robbie and told him what Vaughn and I had planned to do.

"Okay," Robbie said, "Brett's mother already invited me for supper. Is that all right?"

"Perfect. Vaughn and I'll come home after we eat."

I ended the call satisfied that Robbie was content to be more independent. At fourteen, it was time.

Vaughn parked the car in town, and we walked down the

street hand in hand to Ken's, a neighborhood bar in town that served great food. It was a favorite of the locals.

Ken, the owner of the bar, acted as bartender, a job he loved. It was a convenient way for him to collect the news of people in town.

He waved to us when we walked inside. "Back from movieland?" he said to Vaughn.

"Back home. My favorite place to be," said Vaughn wrapping an arm around my shoulder.

Ken waved me over to him.

When I reached him, he leaned over the bar and said softly, "I hear the new owner of Osteria Arno is out to get you and Rhonda. He wants to become the number one place to go for dinner on the Gulf Coast. He's telling everyone you stole his chef."

I sucked in my lips. "If you hear anything else, will you let me know? He wants us to compete, but Rhonda and I aren't about to play any games with him. We don't need to compete. We have our clientele, and they're happy with us."

Though Ken and I were talking softly, Vaughn was able to hear some of the conversation. He gave me a worried look.

I'd been dreading the time when I'd have to tell Vaughn about the harassment Rhonda and I and the hotel were facing. Now, I couldn't avoid it.

Vaughn led me over to a corner booth and we sat down.

"Are you going to tell me what's going on?" said Vaughn. "I don't like what I'm hearing."

The waitress came to our table, and we placed our orders.

After she left, Vaughn said, "So?"

"I told you about hiring Chet and how he was blackballed in Miami by the chef he accused of stealing his recipes," I said.

"Yeah, there shouldn't be any problem doing that," Vaughn said. "So what aren't you telling me?"

"After Rhonda and I worked on the special Italian dinner, I went out to my car to find the tires on it slashed. We think it was Jonny Arno's supporters who did it. Our security team at the hotel now patrols that area and we've had no other incidents like it." I swallowed hard. "But there was no mistaking the venom in Jonny's eyes when he vowed to best Rhonda and me and the hotel."

"He threatened you?" Vaughn hissed in an effort to keep his voice down.

"In a way, he did. But when he spoke to me like that, he'd just been shut down from making a fool of himself over an inappropriate request of the Ambassador. That made him angry at me."

"Have there been any more incidents?" Vaughn asked.

"No," I said. "Bernie, Rhonda, and I agree we won't be drawn into any arguments with him. There really is no need for us to be involved in any."

"I need you to promise me that the minute things get worse between you and him, you'll let me know. I can't stand by quietly while I think you might get hurt." Vaughn gave me a steady look. "Promise?"

"Yes," I said. "I think it's more bluster than anything else. He's an egotistical man who failed miserably in Miami and thinks he can renew his reputation here."

"What does Rhonda think?" Vaughn asked.

"She thinks he's a dick ..." I began and laughed when I saw Vaughn's lips curve.

"Never mind. I get it," he said, chuckling. "One always knows where they stand with Rhonda."

Our beers and burgers came, and then it was quiet while we ate.

"Well, well, if it isn't Ann Grayson and her husband slumming it here."

I choked on my beer and looked up into Jonny's unpleasant sneer.

"I gather you don't know much about the town," said Vaughn. "Ken's has been here for years and is a favorite among the locals."

"Vaughn, this is Jonny Arno," I said with reluctance. He was an obnoxious man who didn't realize what a small town Sabal was. He was heading for political suicide by making fun of some of Sabal's favorite establishments.

Vaughn gave Jonny a long stare and remained seated. "I understand you have shown animosity toward my wife. I don't like it. Understand?"

Jonny's face flushed a bright red. "It's just business competition. That's all. I'm out to prove that my restaurant is going to be known as the best on the west coast of Florida. If she or her partner can't stand the heat, maybe it's time for them to get out of the business."

Ken walked over to us. "Jonny, we have your table set up."

Jonny turned and walked away.

Ken quietly said, "Sorry about that."

"No worries," said Vaughn keeping a lingering look on Jonny's backside. "He's one of the biggest assholes I've ever met."

After Ken left, Vaughn gave me a worried look. "I'm going to speak to Bernie about this. I want him to understand that this man's ego is dangerous."

"Bernie, Rhonda, and I have already discussed this," I said. "We are taking measures to ensure our safety and that of the hotel."

"Good, because I don't trust that man to be decent to anyone," said Vaughn. "How did he ever get to be such a chef celebrity?"

"By using people, according to Chet," I said. "When you

watch some cooking shows, everything is prepared for the chef to use in a recipe. It's a lot of showmanship to make it seem as if the chef is the brilliant one."

"I just don't want anything bad to happen to you," Vaughn said, reaching across the table and taking hold of my hand. "I love you."

My heart filled. "I love you, too. Let's enjoy the time together and not waste another moment on Jonny Arno."

"Deal," said Vaughn. "How about another beer?"

The next morning when I went in to work, I took my time outside in the back parking area to look around. A security guard was in sight, making me feel secure. I decided we were all overreacting to Jonny. Even if he surrounded himself with people we didn't like, he really had no reason to do more than to try to open a spectacular restaurant that took business away from us. Competition was fair.

Inside the hotel, I greeted Consuela then grabbed a cup of coffee and took it into the office.

I was checking over the financials for the last wedding when Rhonda walked in.

"I heard the mother-of-the bride is trying to sue us. I talked to Mike about it, and he said not to worry," said Rhonda. Mike Torson was our lawyer and handled our legal business.

"With all the witness reports and other data, she'd only be embarrassing herself," I said. "But I want to tell you about meeting Jonny yesterday."

After filling Rhonda in on the incident at Ken's, I told her we might be overreacting to Jonny. He was an obnoxious person who would have to work hard to compete with us. "His manner is very abrasive, and his ego knows no bounds, but we can't afford to let him derail our daily business."

"If Vaughn doesn't trust him, neither do I," said Rhonda. "But what else can we do except keep an eye on him?"

"We can do that and work on the new program the girls want to put together with Harper. Thanksgiving will be here in a couple of months, and then everything will go crazy with the holidays and high season."

"Okay. I'm all for it. Are you ready to meet with Lorraine and Annette for a follow-up to the wedding?" said Rhonda.

"I'm all set. It makes such a difference to have Vaughn home. I have more energy."

Rhonda's eyebrows shot up and she gave me a suggestive wagging of her eyebrows.

I raised my hand to stop her from making a comment. "I know where you're going with this and stop."

Rhonda chuckled. "I can't help it. Your voice gets all funny when you talk about Vaughn like that. You two lovebirds..."

I couldn't help my smile.

"You're not the only ones," said Rhonda. "Will and I are planning a little vacation for just the two of us. Just a couple of days this fall. It's the only way we have any time to ourselves. I've ordered a new sexy negligee."

Rhonda and I gave one another a high five. We worked hard, but we knew it was important to play hard, too.

After meeting with Lorraine, Lauren, and Annette to review the past wedding, Rhonda and I decided to go outside onto the beach for a quiet moment together. There was no doubt that weddings brought in a lot of money, especially if we put heads in beds. But the amount of work was considerable. Ever since Lorraine married, her availability had become more divided. It was time to do something different about it. There was no better place to discuss it than on the beach.

I took off my sandals and walked onto the sand, loving the soft feel of it between my toes and on the soles of my feet. I strolled to the water's edge, feeling my body relax as I inhaled the salty, clean air and lifted my arms to the sun above.

At my side, Rhonda let out a groan of pleasure. "It always feels so relaxing to be here, huh?"

Above us, seagulls and terns were circling in the air, their white wings distinct against the deep blue sky. Below us, the waves wove lacy patterns on the sand, marred only by the tiny footprints left behind by the shore birds searching for food.

"Who'd a thunk we'd be so successful, Annie?" Rhonda said. "If we hadn't met, I would never have been able to make this hotel happen."

"I had to make it succeed to prove to Robert I could survive without him," I said, remembering the difficulties I'd had getting my share of money to invest.

"We both had something to prove," said Rhonda, walking along the sand beside me. "Now, what are we going to do about the wedding business? We've given Annette and Lauren new titles, and Lorraine will continue to be involved, but should we bring someone else on board?"

"I think we should," I said. "Maybe start someone part-time to be on hand for the actual wedding party in house. Someone to follow through on the details that have already been worked out."

"I was wondering if that's something Harper might like to do in addition to bartending," said Rhonda. "She's very ambitious and a great people person."

"That's something to think about," I agreed. "I like her."

We turned around to head back to the hotel and stopped in surprise when we saw Chet and Philippa walking toward us hand in hand.

Rhonda snapped to attention. "Well, what do we have here? A chance for me to put my matchmaking skills to use?"

"Now, Rhonda," I began, but I couldn't stop the grin of excitement spreading across her face.

Rhonda waved and hurried forward to greet them. "Fancy seeing you here together. Beautiful day."

"Yes, " said Philippa. "It's a lovely morning. My mother left earlier to return to New York for some social affairs with my father. She'll return to the house we're staying in as soon as she can. I hope that's all right."

"No worries," said Rhonda. "Emergencies like that sometimes happen to our guests. So, I guess you two are getting reacquainted."

Chet's lips curved. "We've had a chance to talk."

"We've talked a lot. There's nothing like the beauty of The Beach House Hotel to help someone relax and enjoy their time here," said Philippa.

"Absolutely. I think so too," said Rhonda.

"Is there anything you need while you stay here by yourself at the guesthouse?" I asked.

"No, thanks," said Philippa. "Harper is going to move into the guesthouse with me. My mother insisted that she'd feel better about leaving if she knew I had company."

I bet, I thought, saying nothing. The thought of Chet and Philippa staying together might be a bit unsettling to her.

"How are things going in the kitchen?" I asked Chet.

"Great. It was super busy with the wedding, and I learned a lot. Today is my day off."

Rhonda gave him a nod of approval. "We like to hear that our employees are taking their job seriously. Enjoy your time together."

Chet and Philippa glanced at one another.

I guided Rhonda away from them. When we were far

enough away, I said to her, "I don't think we should be encouraging the two of them. Remember, Philippa told us about a family commitment of sorts."

Rhonda put her hand on her hip and shook her head. "Baloney! That's nonsense in this day and age. You can see these two young people are in love. It looks like they never forgot one another after meeting in New York. I, for one, am not going to stand in the way of love."

I rolled my eyes and sighed. "I just don't want more trouble."

"Aw, Annie. Whenever I see a spark of love, I want to help it grow into something more. I can't help myself. And what I saw between the two of them was a lot more than a spark."

"I'm glad Harper will be staying at the guesthouse," I said. "That will make it less worrisome. Speaking of Harper, let's go see if she's at the apartment."

CHAPTER THIRTEEN

RHONDA AND I KNOCKED ON THE DOOR OF THE APARTMENT where Chet and Harper were staying.

Moments later, Harper appeared wearing shorts and a T-shirt, looking surprised to see us. "Hello."

" 'Morning," I said. "Do you have some time to talk?"

"Sure. Is everything all right?" Harper replied.

"Very much so. We might have a new opportunity for you."

"Oh. Please come in," said Harper. "I'm sorry the place is in a bit of a mess. I'm packing to move into the guesthouse with Philippa for a few days."

"We ran into Philippa and Chet walking on the beach together, and they mentioned that," said Rhonda as we moved inside. "They sure looked cute together."

"I heard about Philippa from Chet before we even came here," said Harper. "They spent a night together in New York City, and he's never forgotten her. It seems like fate has given them a second chance. It's so sweet."

"Maybe not," I said taking a seat on the couch. "Her family thinks Philippa might be bound by a family agreement to marry someone from home."

"Oh," said Harper. "I hadn't heard that."

I switched the topic. "Rhonda and I are wondering if you'd be interested in doing part-time work during weddings, helping to act as a liaison between the hotel staff and the wedding party. You're very good with people."

"Thank you," said Harper taking a seat at the other end of the couch from me. "This would be in addition to my bartending?"

"Yes," said Rhonda. "Your wedding work would be outside of your hours at the bar. We think you have potential for growth within the hotel."

Harper gave us a thoughtful look. "Let me think about it."

"Okay, " I said, getting to my feet. "If you're interested, come see us at the office before you go to work this afternoon and we'll talk particulars. We didn't want to proceed until we knew you were interested."

Rhonda and I said goodbye to Harper and walked to our office talking about various options for someone like Harper.

At our desks, we quickly agreed on a salary for her and a possible schedule then set it aside for a later conversation with her.

"Now that we've got that settled, we can relax," said Rhonda.

"I hope so. The wedding next weekend is small and should be easy to handle. A pleasant way for Harper to be introduced."

"And the group luncheons this week are pretty light," Rhonda said, leaning back in her chair. "Maybe Will and I should try to get away this week. Would you mind, Annie?"

"No, it seems like a quiet time. Where are you thinking of going?"

"To an inn in North Carolina. The mountains should be pretty and cool at this time of year," said Rhonda.

"Sounds lovely," I said. "Perfect for a short get-away."

The phone rang.

I picked it up. "Hello. Oh, hi, Lindsay, what's up?" I listened, becoming more and more horrified.

Rhonda grabbed my arm. "What is it?"

"Hold on, Lindsay." I turned to Rhonda. "Jean-Luc has had a fall and broken his ankle. He's on bedrest until they can get the swelling in his foot to go down and put a cast on him."

"Oh, no," said Rhonda.

I returned to the call and listened as Lindsay gave me more information. But I had enough to know we were in a real mess. "Thanks for the call," I managed to say to Lindsay. "Tell Jean-Luc not to worry, we'll figure something out."

Rhonda let out a loud sigh. "What are we going to do?"

"Find Chet," I said.

"And call Bernie," said Rhonda.

When I tried to call Chet, I got his voice message. Frustrated with his lack of response, I trotted over to the guesthouse where Philippa was staying. I didn't have her cell number, so it was the only way to try and reach him.

I stood outside the front door and waited for someone to answer my knock.

Philippa came to the door dripping wet from the pool. She frowned when she saw me. "Hi, Ann."

"Is Chet here?" I asked her. "I tried to call him, but it went straight to voice message. It's important."

"Come on in. He's here."

"I'm sorry to interrupt, but like I said, it's important."

Chet was lying on his back in a chaise lounge asleep.

I went up to him and shook him gently. "Chet, wake up. I need to talk to you."

His eyes flashed open. "Wha?"

"We've had an emergency at the hotel. Jean-Luc broke his ankle, and he's on bedrest at home. We need you to come into the kitchen right away."

Chet jumped to his feet, wide awake now. "When did this happen?"

"Apparently, last night. I'll have more information later.

Right now, we have a crisis on our hands. The wedding breakfast is going on now and we have a fully booked dining room for dinner tonight."

Chet pulled on a pair of shorts over his bathing suit, grabbed his shirt and sandals and gave Philippa a hug. "I'll check in with you later, Phil."

"Is there any way I can help?" she asked me.

"Possibly," I said. "I'll let you know. Harper is going to come talk to Rhonda and me after she gets settled here at the house. Why don't you come with her?"

"Okay. I'd be happy to help in whatever way I can," she replied with eagerness.

Chet and I walked to the hotel and went directly to the kitchen. Rhonda and Bernie were with the kitchen staff.

"Fortunately," Bernie was saying. "You all have been well-trained by Jean-Luc to do your jobs." He looked at us. "And we have a new chef on board who will be able to help oversee the kitchen during this period of recovery for Jean-Luc. I want you all to respect his authority. He, with Ricardo's help, will take on Jean-Luc's role until he's able to return."

Rhonda and I glanced at one another with approval. Ricardo Perez was a sous chef who'd been with us a number of years and was loyal to the hotel. He would understand the need for him to continue in his role while helping Chet.

"For this last minute change in menu, we'll need to come up with an idea for dinner this evening," said Ricardo. "Going forward, we'll take it one day at a time. Jean-Luc has his special dishes which I don't think we should mess with."

"I agree," I said. "Why don't we do something entirely different? We could offer a special prix fixe Italian menu along with our usual menu."

"Chet can handle that, can't you?" Rhonda asked him.

"Yes," said Chet straightening. "Ricardo and I will work on the selections and give you a menu to approve."

"Right," agreed Ricardo.

"Great," said Bernie. "Bring it to me ASAP and we'll see if we can get some publicity for it."

"Terri Thomas at Sabal Daily News owes us a favor," I said. "It's too late for tonight, but maybe we'll be able to offer it tomorrow, too."

"A different way to add to our business," said Rhonda.

"Okay. Looks like we have a plan. I must get back to overseeing the departure of our wedding guests, especially the parents of the bride," said Bernie.

After he left, I turned to the kitchen crew. "Let's make Jean-Luc proud."

"Yes," said Rhonda. "You can do it."

As Chet and Ricardo headed for Jean-Luc's office, the rest of the staff scattered in the kitchen. Jean-Luc had insisted that everyone know their job and at least one other in case of an emergency like this.

Rhonda and I went to our office and sat down facing one another.

"This is going to be a true test not only for Chet and Ricardo, but for the entire staff," said Rhonda. "I didn't want to mention it in front of the others, but do you think it's wise for us to offer a special Italian meal?"

"Do you mean in light of our disagreement with Jonny Arno?" I asked.

Rhonda shrugged. "What if our Italian menu becomes something our guests want us to continue?"

I could feel my temper rising. I'd been so careful in my first marriage not to annoy my ex. It had kept me from doing what I wanted. I couldn't let that happen again. Rhonda and I had the right to do what was necessary with our business.

Rhonda chuckled and waggled a finger at me. "You don't have to say a word. I see the expression on your face and have your answer. You're right. We shouldn't be worried about it."

A knock on the door diverted our attention.

"Come in," said Rhonda.

Harper and Philippa walked in.

"Harper, please have a seat," I said. "Philippa, follow me. You might be able to help Chet and Ricardo with a special menu."

When Philippa and I approached Jean-Luc's office, Chet and Ricardo were working on a computer.

"I thought you gentlemen might want some help. Philippa could have some ideas for you."

"Great," said Chet. "Ricardo, this is Philippa Ferrara. Phil, this is Ricardo Perez, the sous chef.

"I'll leave you to it," I said, not wanting to interfere any more than I had.

In the office, Rhonda and Harper were talking about our wedding business.

I took a seat and listened to what Rhonda was saying about our growth in that area and how Lorraine wasn't able to devote as much time to it.

"Anything to add, Annie?" Rhonda asked.

"You explained it well," I said. "What we're looking for is someone like yourself, Harper, to work a few hours on the weekends we have a wedding in-house to trail a wedding group, making sure they have what they need. You'd be following plans that were already made and some that might be spontaneous. It wouldn't be for every wedding, depending on size and group activities. We'd make sure there'd be no loss of pay if it affected bartending time."

"Would I do this alone?" asked Harper.

"You'd be part of the wedding team but would have no responsibility in making the plans," I explained. "You'd help see that those plans were successful. Lauren is an assistant to Lorraine Grace, who manages weddings with Annette Bruner. But she can't always do her job and tag the group."

"For instance, the mother-of-the-bride in our last wedding fell by the pool," said Rhonda. "If someone had checked in with that group occasionally, perhaps some kind of intervention might have happened."

"I know from working in the bar that the last wedding group consisted of a bunch of drinkers who could be difficult to deal with," said Harper. "Are they all like that?"

"Absolutely not," Rhonda said. "But even easy-going groups need to have someone they can turn to for help from time to time. The reason we thought of you is that you seem to fit in with most groups because you're friendly and naturally helpful."

"It's something to think about," I said. "We have a small group wedding next weekend so probably don't need your help until the wedding following it."

"Thank you. I am interested. I like the hospitality business and want to learn what I can," said Harper. "I especially want to work with your daughters on helping to pull in a younger crowd for happy hours."

"Superb. They want to do that with you," I said. "As busy mothers, they don't have many free hours, but they know that one day they'll take over for us and want to keep active in the business as much as possible."

"Just as you'd do for weddings, you can be the person to help things along with projects for the girls. It's something the three of you should discuss," said Rhonda.

A wide smile stretched across Harper's face. "I like that idea a lot. Thank you for thinking of me."

"We'll set up a time for you to meet with Lorraine and Lauren," I said.

Harper rose. "Thank you again. I'll wait to hear when you want me to meet with the wedding department."

She left the office, and Rhonda and I faced one another.

"Just another day at the hotel, huh?" Rhonda teased.

I laughed. "A day like so many others."

Chet, Ricardo, and Philippa brought a copy of the menu they'd given Bernie to us.

After looking at it, I was impressed. "It's simple but allows a varied selection of food."

"It's very typical of a Sunday dinner in Italy," said Philippa. "But it won't be family style."

"There's nothing that we can't handle," Ricardo said. "Phil has even offered to consult with the antipasti. And we have the food on hand but will need to order more for tomorrow."

"Okay, then. As long as Bernie has approved, type up the menu and print it on heavy stock paper to be added to our regular dinner menus," I said. "It's a fair price for the four course meal."

"I agree," said Rhonda. "With a choice of two main courses and two desserts, it should sell well."

"The wine package is something that Bernie approved," said Chet. "With a choice of four different wines, it should please everyone, with wines for each course."

I checked my watch. "Time to get to it."

"How is the rest of the day going, Chet?" Rhonda asked.

"We checked before we came here. We're on schedule, thanks to Ricardo."

Ricardo gave Chet a little salute, and then the three of them left the office.

"That chicken piccata sounds delicious," Rhonda said. "Guess I'd better grab something for lunch. Who knows when we'll have another chance if the day continues like this."

We walked into the kitchen and went over to Consuela. "How did the breakfast go?"

"Fine," she said. "I've got a cooperative team for breakfast and lunch. What's happening with dinner with Jean-Luc gone?"

We filled her in on the Italian special.

"Even the Ambassador's daughter is helping out," said Rhonda. "It couldn't work better for my matchmaking skills."

Consuela and I glanced at each other and laughed.

"Now, now. You know my rate of success is very high," said Rhonda seriously. "Did you notice the way Philippa and Chet stared at one another, Annie? I'm tellin' ya, it's a very hot romance in the making."

"What about the person Philippa is supposed to marry? said Consuela. "You told me all about him."

"I don't think it'll ever happen," said Rhonda stubbornly.

I shook my head. I thought the situation was a lot more complicated. But I, like Rhonda, would have to wait and see.

CHAPTER FOURTEEN

AFTER SPLITTING A CLUB SANDWICH IN THE OFFICE, Rhonda and I decided to make a visit to Jean-Luc. We wanted to see for ourselves how bad his injuries were.

"I'll drive," said Rhonda.

We got into her car, a vintage Cadillac convertible Rhonda loved, and took off for a neighborhood north of Sabal. Though the houses were older and smaller than the massive ones in the developments on either side of it, these sat right next to the beach in a sheltered cove. A prime location that outdid its neighbors.

I called Lindsay on the way to alert her to our arrival.

"He'll be glad to see you," she said. "He's very irritated that he can't be at the hotel."

"How bad is the injury?" I asked.

"Not as bad as a complete break. If he has his way he'll be back in the kitchen in a day or two. We'll see."

I ended the call and turned to Rhonda. "We'll have to be diplomatic talking to Jean-Luc. We want him to know we can handle his absence for now, but we can't give him the impression he's not missed. You know how sensitive, he is."

"You're right. If he comes back to work too soon and then has to stay out longer to recover, that will really hurt us," Rhonda said as we pulled into the driveway of Jean-Luc's house.

I got out of the car and stood a moment to gaze at the two-story stucco structure with a red tile roof. It was charming in a way that some of the larger houses were not.

Rhonda and I walked up to the front door, rang the bell, and waited for Lindsay to greet us.

The door opened and a boy of about four grinned at us. "Here's Mommy."

Lindsay stood behind him and wrapped her arm around his shoulder. "*Merci,* Jacques. Welcome Ann and Rhonda. Please come in. The patient is in the den."

We walked inside and followed Lindsay to a room that held one wall of bookshelves.

Lying on the couch, facing a large television screen, Jean-Luc looked up at us and grimaced. "I'm sorry. Such a stupid thing to do."

"What happened?" I asked. "We didn't get the details."

"I was climbing a ladder to put in a new lightbulb, and it tipped over. I fell on my right ankle."

"You could've been hurt much worse," said Rhonda. "Don't worry. We've got the kitchen covered."

"But we want you back as soon as you're ready," I said, seeing the flash of alarm cross Jean-Luc's face.

"Who's handling things? Ricardo?" he asked.

"Ricardo and Chet are teaming up together. Tonight, and tomorrow, we're offering a special prix fixe Italian dinner. Ricardo didn't want to mess with a few specials of yours."

"Thanks for that," said Jean-Luc. "The doctor doesn't want me on my feet until the swelling goes down. Then he'll see about a cast or surgery."

"Jean-Luc's willing to do anything, even lie on the couch with ice packs, to move things along," said Lindsay. "You know how hard that is for him to do." She stroked the back of Jean-Luc's neck and his expression softened with love.

A child cried in another room. "Excuse me," said Lindsay. "I have to go get Damon."

"We can't stay," I said. "But we had to make sure Jean-Luc

is all right. He's an important part of our hotel family."

Lindsay's lips curved. "Yes, I know. No one, not even Jonny Arno can compare to him."

Jean-Luc chuckled. "Wait until Jonny sees you're putting on an Italian dinner. When is his restaurant due to open?"

"In a couple of days," said Rhonda. "Guess who hasn't received an invitation to the grand opening?"

"Bah! We don't need to be there," Jean-Luc said, curling his lips. "We know it will be a ... how do you call it? ... a shit show."

"Probably." I leaned over and kissed him on the cheek. "Get well soon. We miss you."

Rhonda came over to him and squeezed his hand. "It's not the same without you."

We left the house, and instead of driving back to the hotel, Rhonda headed north.

"Where are you going?" I asked.

"I want to get a look at Osteria Arno. I've purposely stayed away, but now might be time to take a gander at our so-called competition," said Rhonda.

"I don't want to be seen spying there," I said, wishing we weren't in Rhonda's flamboyant car.

"I do. I want Jonny's team to know we're not afraid to be seen," said Rhonda. "Remember, I grew up in a neighborhood where some of the guys were similar to Jonny. Big, loud bullies."

A few miles down the road we turned away from the beach and drove through a stone entryway for Osteria Arno. We cruised up to the front of a building still undergoing finishing touches.

"Wow, Annie! Would you look at that?" Rhonda gaped at it

and turned to me wide-eyed.

I shook my head, unable to believe that something so garish was our so-called competition. The white wooden structure had a white stone front with four fake wooden columns, two on each side of wide double doors painted bright pink with gold trim and accents.

From the side of the building, Brock Goodwin saw us and came meandering over, wearing a self-satisfied smile. "Couldn't stay away, huh?"

"We were curious," I said.

"Curiosity killed the cat, you know," said Brock.

"Aw, we're not afraid of you," said Rhonda, settling her gaze on the restaurant. "And it looks as if we needn't be afraid of any competition from Jonny."

"Jonny hired an architect who's done some work in South Beach," Brock said proudly. "The pink doors reflect the famous Gulf Coast sunsets. And the columns represent the importance of the people behind the operation."

I gave Rhonda a warning look. God knew what she would say to all that. "What's the theme inside?"

"Pretty much the same," said Brock. "The decorator is a friend of the architects."

Jonny pulled into the parking lot and drove right past us.

"See ya later," said Rhonda. "We've got a meeting."

We made it as far as the road before we burst out laughing.

By the time we made it back to the hotel, we'd gone from laughter to worry.

"If the appearance of the restaurant is an indication of the quality of food inside, I don't see how Jonny is going to make it," I said.

Rhonda made a face. "I know. And he's going to want to

blame us for his failing."

I checked my watch. "Terri Thomas should be at the hotel soon. We shouldn't say anything to her about seeing Jonny's restaurant. We have to simply promote our new prix fixe menu."

"Right. I don't think I could mention it without wanting to laugh or cry," said Rhonda, and I suddenly realized we might be in more trouble than I'd thought.

We'd maintained a cordial relationship with Terri Thomas at Sabal Daily News through the years by making sure she felt special at the hotel. That feeling included warm cinnamon rolls, cookies, or some other treats. Today, we were going to offer her a sample of a few canapés we were showcasing at the bar. An older woman who'd worked for the paper for years, she missed nothing.

When Terri arrived, we greeted her warmly and suggested we go into the dining room to meet. The restaurant wouldn't open for another hour, and we'd have privacy to talk.

At a prearranged signal, a member of the kitchen staff brought a small plate to Terri.

"We thought you might enjoy some canapés while we talk," I said. "What can we get you to drink with that?"

"I'd love a glass of white wine. You women are always so welcoming, thank you," Terri said, beaming at us.

"We like to think we're welcoming to each of our guests," said Rhonda. "But we want to talk business with you, too."

"Yes," I said. "Your article about Osteria Arno was something that gave us cause to worry. We're not in any special competition with that restaurant. We welcome any chef to the area, very confident that we don't have to prove ourselves. Not with Jean-Luc's sterling reputation."

"He's an excellent teacher as well," said Rhonda.

"And generous," I added. "His new chef, Chet Waring, is presenting a prix fixe meal tonight and tomorrow. A special dinner offering while Jean-Luc recovers from a broken ankle."

Rhonda leaned forward. "We'd really appreciate your support on this, Terri. We figure that after highlighting Osteria Arno, you'd be willing to help us spread the word."

"Besides, we always like to give you a heads-up on some of the things going on at the hotel," I said. "Sometimes even special interviews with celebrities." I'd arranged a few for her with guests who wanted the publicity.

Terri lifted a small piece of toasted bread ladened with smoked salmon and a dab of sour cream, topped with a couple of capers and slid it into her mouth. "Mmm," she uttered, taking a sip of wine. "What a delight for late afternoon."

"We're changing up our bar tasting menu with a few more canapé choices that might attract a younger set of foodies to it," said Rhonda. "You know how much we love our food."

"Indeed, I do," said Terri, reaching for a cracker topped with paté.

"So, will you help us?" I asked. "We have a printed menu to give you. We'd appreciate a positive recommendation. If you'd like, you can invite a guest for dinner tomorrow night to sample it."

Terri swallowed her second cracker. "Okay. But first, I need to ask you—have you talked to Jonny Arno? Are you invited to the soft opening in two days? The official opening to the public will be next Saturday."

"The answer to both questions is no," said Rhonda.

Terri leaned back and gazed at us. "I thought so. He doesn't strike me as the kind of person to play fair."

"That's why we need your help," I said.

Terri took a look at the menu I handed her. "Why an Italian

menu? Isn't that a slap in the face for Jonny?"

"Chet has a ready menu of Italian food. We needed to come up with something quick because of Jean-Luc's accident. That doesn't mean he can't cook anything else," said Rhonda.

"We hope to have prix fixe meals every once in a while," I said. "Not all of them with an Italian flare."

Terri let out a sigh and picked up her wine glass. "Okay, I'll do it. But only because Jonny didn't invite me to his private, soft opening party. I'm always invited to them."

"Thanks," said Rhonda. "We've been supporting one another for years. It seems only right that we continue that relationship regardless of what other restaurants are in the area."

"We don't wish harm to anyone else," I said. "We just want to be able to carry on with our own business."

"As you should be able to do and without interference." Terri stood. "I'll bring a guest with me tomorrow night. Thanks for the delicious refreshments and the glass of wine. As always, you women know how to woo me."

Grinning, Rhonda and I walked her through the lobby to the front door.

Rhonda and I went to check on progress for dinner. Monday nights in the dining room were usually slower than the rest of the week, but our hotel was full, which meant we'd be busy.

In the kitchen, everything was surprisingly in order. Chet and Ricardo seemed very calm as staff members worked at their stations. Philippa had changed into jeans and a T-shirt like the rest of the crew and was wearing a long, white apron over them.

I went to her. "How's it going?"

"Fine. I like doing work like this. It reminds me of being in my nonna's kitchen preparing the family Sunday dinner," she answered, giving me a bright smile.

"We appreciate your help. We'll settle the paperwork later," I said, wondering how Philippa's parents would feel about their daughter consulting in our kitchen. Maybe, after this crisis, we could place her in the hospitality group.

Chet came over to us. "It looks like it'll be a busy night in the dining room. We posted the prix fixe menu outside the dining room and the reservations are coming in. But no worries. Ricardo and I have everything ready for the entire menu."

"Thanks," said Rhonda. "How does it feel to be in charge?"

"It feels nice," said Chet. "Tell Jean-Luc he's trained his staff well."

"He runs a disciplined kitchen," I said, delighted to see how well Chet was handling the situation.

"One more stop," said Rhonda, "and then I'm going home."

"I'll be right behind you. Vaughn is cooking dinner tonight."

When we walked into the lobby lounge to speak to Harper, we saw her behind the bar talking to a young man with dark curly hair, broad shoulders, and a muscular body.

We called out to Harper, and he turned to face us.

I couldn't help staring at one of the most handsome men I'd ever seen. Even from a few steps away, I was drawn to his bright blue, almost green, eyes fringed by thick eyelashes. They stood in contrast to his chiseled features.

Harper came from behind the bar and walked over to us. "Hi." She turned to the young man. "Ann Sanders and Rhonda Grayson are the owners of the hotel." She beamed at us. "Ann and Rhonda, meet Luciano Bolino. He's here to surprise Philippa."

Luciano's white smile widened as he shook our hands. "Actually, Philippa's father, Enrico Ferrara, suggested I pay his daughter a visit. A family situation."

CHAPTER FIFTEEN

IT TOOK ME A MINUTE TO REMEMBER WHERE I'D HEARD that name and realized Luciano must be the man meant for Philippa. "Did you explain that Philippa was busy at the moment?" I asked Harper.

"Luciano just walked in, so we didn't get much of a chance to talk," said Harper. She turned to Luciano. "Wait here, I'll notify Philippa."

As Harper rushed away, Rhonda and I exchanged worried looks.

A few minutes later, Harper appeared alone. "Philippa asks Luciano to meet her in the kitchen staff room. They'll have privacy there."

"Staff room?" said Luciano looking surprised.

Rather than try to explain, I led Luciano to the private room.

Philippa met us at the door and threw her arms around Luciano. "Hello, old friend. What brought you here?"

He hugged her. "Actually, your father did. He suggested I make the journey here to see you because your mother has delayed the family trip to Italy."

Frowning, Phillipa stepped away from Luciano. "Oh, dear. Is this about our grandfathers and their wish for us to marry? I'm glad you're here so we can get this settled for all time. Neither one of us wants to dishonor them, but we're going to have to face our *nonnos* and tell them how we really feel. It was a sweet idea that isn't going to happen. I thought they knew that."

"I tried to tell your father the old family idea was not ever going to work and then decided it was better if it came from both of us. Besides, I've always wanted to see Florida."

Harper popped her head inside. "Everything okay?"

Philippa put her arm around Harper and said to Luciano, "This is my new roommate. Harper Lewis. She'll be glad to show you around while I work for the next couple of days." She glanced at Harper. "You'll do it, won't you?"

Harper's cheeks turned a pink color almost as bright as her strawberry-blond hair, and she nodded.

"You have a choice," Philippa said to Luciano. "You can stay in the guesthouse with Harper and me or move in with my friend, Chet Waring, one of the chefs. He's staying in an apartment right here on the property."

"Staying with Chet is a great idea," I interjected, already wary of problems arising with Philippa's parents.

"I'm happy to stay anywhere you want to put me," Luciano said politely, "but I want plenty of time to be able to talk privately with you, Philippa."

We turned as Chet knocked and entered. "Hey, Phil, we need you." He stopped and looked over the crowd, resting his gaze on Luciano. "Sorry, I didn't mean to interrupt."

"It's okay," said Philippa. "I want you to meet Luciano Bolino, my childhood friend. He's visiting for a while."

Chet smiled and gripped Luciano's hand. "Welcome."

"Thanks." Luciano's gaze switched to Philippa and back to Chet.

"I truly am glad you came," said Philippa, rising on her toes to give Luciano a kiss on the cheek before leaving with Chet.

Rhonda knocked and came into the room.

I knew her so well I could see her mind racing with all kinds of matchmaking possibilities. I sighed. If Rhonda had her way, she'd somehow make something romantic work between the four of them.

Harper said to Luciano, "Okay, I said I'd help you and give you a tour. Where's your luggage? Let's get it and get you settled. But first, I need to check in with my boss and let him know I'll be gone for a short while."

"No worries. I'll tell him," Rhonda said. "You go ahead and make sure Luciano feels welcome."

As they walked away, Rhonda grinned at me. "I just might be able to help two couples at once."

"You can only do so much," I said. "But it does seem as if Luciano came to Florida to settle things between Philippa and him."

"He's adorable," said Rhonda. "But Harper with her pretty hair and green eyes is cute as a button. They'd make an adorable match."

I faced her. "We have to be very careful not to influence any person in that foursome because we have parents who care a lot. Maybe too much."

"Okay, okay. I get it," said Rhonda. She clasped her hands and winked at me. "Oh, to be young again. Such challenges lie ahead for them."

I flung my arm around Rhonda's shoulder. "C'mon. Time to go. I'll check in with Annette later to see how the meal is going, but I want to be home with Vaughn. I never know when his work will take him away again."

When I pulled into my driveway, I noticed Stephanie and Randolph Willis's car parked to one side. I was happy for the chance to spend time with them.

One Christmas, when the hotel was too full to accommodate them, I'd invited them to stay at my home. They'd been Robbie's adopted grandparents ever since and had easily become a part of my family. For someone who'd grown up with a cold, perfectionist grandmother, they, like Consuela and Manny, were like parents to me.

I got out of the car and eagerly headed inside.

Cindy greeted me and then raced away to Randolph who was sitting on the lanai. "Hello," I said, hugging Stephanie and then Randolph. "What a nice surprise."

Vaughn kissed me and said, "We met at Robbie's swim practice, and I invited them for dinner. I'm grilling some steaks."

"A delightful suggestion," I said. "I'll change my clothes and join you."

"I'll help with dinner in any way I can," said Stephanie. In her early seventies, she was healthy and active.

"Great. We can gab in the kitchen," I said. "There's so much to tell you."

"If it's about Jonny Arno, I have news for you too," said Stephanie.

I checked in with Robbie, who was playing video games in his room and went to change.

A few moments later, I met with Stephanie in the kitchen. Vaughn had poured her a glass of red wine and left a glass of it for me.

I lifted my glass and clinked it against Stephanie's. "I'm glad you're here. How's our boy doing with his swimming?"

Stephanie chuckled. "Robbie has a natural ability to do well. And his long arms help." "Spoken like a true grandmother," I teased. Stephanie had tried for children of her own and had had miscarriages. Robbie and his friends helped fill a previous empty part of her and Randolph's lives.

I handed a head of lettuce to Stephanie, and she went about cleaning it for a salad while I quickly made my special garlic and blue cheese dressing.

"What did you want to tell me about Jonny Arno? I asked her.

"We were invited to a soft opening for a select group in the neighborhood. I'm certain Brock Goodwin is the one who provided him names because several of our friends in the same condo building were invited too."

"How was it? Were many people there? Was the food good?" I asked, unable to stop myself.

Stephanie laughed. "Hang on. I'll tell you about it. But first, who is the chef he's claiming you stole from him."

I filled Stephanie in on the details of hiring Chet Waring and how he came to Sabal. "He's talented, hardworking, and flexible. We're delighted to have him. Especially now that Jean-Luc has broken his ankle."

"Oh, dear!" Stephanie exclaimed. "What are you going to do about that?"

"Chet and Ricardo are handling the kitchen staff. They're a great team and are working together. They've come up with a special prix fixe meal which is serving as a test program for others. The only complication there is that the meal is Italian because of Chet's experience with Italian food and the ability to have an actual Italian person to help with the meal."

"Oh, but Jonny will be angry about that," said Stephanie. "He's a particularly unpleasant man. He wore his chef's uniform for the opening, but I can't see how he did much of the cooking. He spent his time drinking and talking to all of us."

"He thinks of himself as a celebrity chef who deserves all the attention for work done by others. That's how Chet explained it. How was the food?"

"Very good," said Stephanie. "But a little fussy, if you know what I mean. All rich sauces and lots of seasoning. Jean-Luc's meals are so much more ... genuine. Does that make sense?"

"Yes, it does. Subtlety is important, giving one a tasty surprise."

Stephanie gave me a steady look. "Don't aggravate Jonny, sweetie. Promise?"

"Rhonda, Bernie, and I have talked about it. We're not in competition with Jonny. We have our own style, our own success to maintain," I said. "But we don't want to irritate him. Rhonda and I want to keep as far away from him as possible."

Vaughn entered the kitchen. "More wine for the ladies?"

Stephanie and I held out our glasses.

"We'll join you men soon. We're just about done here," I said. "I'll ask Robbie to set the table." Vaughn and I thought it was important for Robbie to participate in entertaining by doing such things. We were a family.

Later, lying in bed with Vaughn, I snuggled up against him and listened as he shared his concerns about Jonny. "Randolph said he's known men like him and doesn't like the idea of him opening a restaurant here. He thinks the mafia is part of the operation, either in the supply chain or with the real estate."

"You know that can happen in the hospitality industry and others," I said. "Until now, I've never had any worrisome thoughts about it. But Jonny is a vindictive kind of person and he's under a lot of pressure."

Vaughn studied me. "Ann, you promise me you'll speak to someone outside your hotel security team about your concerns."

"I will. Let me talk to Roberto Gonzales in our security team about who'd be best to approach. It will make me feel better, too." I lifted my face to kiss him, and all talk of security disappeared.

CHAPTER SIXTEEN

THE NEXT MORNING, AS I OFTEN DID WHEN VAUGHN was home and able to see Robbie off to school, I drove to the hotel to walk along the shore. The calmness I found there gave me a few moments to catch my breath and see things more clearly.

It looked as if it was going to be a stormy day, as the weather reports indicated. Quieter than usual on the beach, I headed off, walking briskly. After several minutes, I stopped to take in the scenery. As usual, the waves with their predictable rhythm soothed my troubled thoughts. Today, when the edge of the wave met the sand, it was with a bit of a slap rather than a caress.

I looked up at the gray sky, seeing the fast moving clouds and knew it would be a difficult day at the hotel, with guests milling around, complaining. Luckily, Lauren, in the events department, would post a list of suggestions for hotel guests to do in town. This might be another way Harper could fit into that department.

Checking my watch, I headed back to the hotel.

As I approached, I noticed Philippa and Luciano talking.

Philippa called, " 'Morning, Ann."

I waved and walked over to them. " 'Morning. How are you?"

Luciano gave me a little bow. "Nice to see you."

"We were just talking about Luciano's stay," said Philippa. "We're not sure how long he'll be visiting, and we want to make it as comfortable for him as possible."

"It depends on so many things." Luciano turned as Harper arrived. "Harper is doing a great job of showing me around. I really appreciate it." The smile he gave Harper made it clear he was interested in more than tours with her.

Harper beamed at him. "We had fun last night after I got off work."

"I'll see you all later," said Philippa. "I promised Chet that I'd wake him this morning. We stayed up late last night talking."

"Before you go, tell me about the special dinner. Were the guests pleased with it?" I asked her.

"It was a huge success. Guests wondered if they could sign up for a prix fixe meal next week," said Philippa. "We explained this was something special, but they could check with you and Rhonda for future possibilities."

"Great answer. We have to be careful how to handle the situation with Jean-Luc," I said. "And we would want to offer different international choices."

"Speaking of Jean-Luc," said Philippa. "Lindsay brought him to the hotel in a wheelchair to see for himself how things are going. As soon as he's fitted to a walking apparatus, he's going to come back to work."

"You can't keep a chef like him away from his kitchen," I said. "Thank you for being such a help. We still need to fill out papers for your work, and we want to talk to you about another opportunity."

"That's what I was telling Luc," Philippa said. "I like it here and have no intention of going back to Italy anytime soon."

I quickly glanced at Luciano.

"Philippa is right," he said. "There's no romance between us no matter what our families want. We have other interests."

"Have you told your families?" I asked.

"Not in so many words," said Luciano. 'I promised

Philippa's father I would discuss the situation with her, and I have. No one wants to dishonor our grandparents."

"Luciano is like a beloved brother to me," said Philippa. She checked her watch. "I really must go."

I stood by with Luciano and Harper as she left.

"It's all right," said Luciano watching her. "It was not meant to be."

"Have a great day, you two," I said and walked away hoping Rhonda and I wouldn't be criticized for allowing Chet and Philippa to work together, as if promoting their relationship.

I stopped in the kitchen before going home to get news from the staff about the dinner and to hopefully get some treats for Vaughn and Robbie.

Consuela and I hugged hello. "Any chance I can take a couple of sweet rolls home to Vaughn?"

She chuckled. "Is that lovely husband of yours home again? How nice. They will be a gift from me to him. I'll get them ready."

I walked to the main kitchen and saw Ricardo.

He came over to me. " 'Morning. How are you?"

"Fine, thanks. I heard the special prix fixe dinner was a success."

A broad smile crossed Ricardo's face. "It was a *big* success. I hope you and Rhonda and Jean-Luc decide to do this often. We have a list of people who want to come back for another one like it."

"We'll have to see about it," I said. "I heard Jean-Luc stopped by."

"He couldn't stay away," said Ricardo. "He told me to expect him back to work in another day or so, that he can guide us from his office or on a special scooter."

We exchanged amused glances.

"I'll leave you to today's activities," I said.

"Chet is taking the morning off, but will be in at noon," said Ricardo. "Tomorrow, I will do the same."

"Whatever schedule you want to work is fine with me," I said. "As long as our hotel meals don't suffer."

Back at home, Vaughn and Robbie were pleased to have Consuela's cinnamon rolls with their breakfast while I got cleaned up to go to work.

I was just inserting pearl earrings into my ear lobes when my cell phone rang. *Rhonda.*

"Hi, what's up?" I asked her.

"I'm here at the office and just ended a conversation with one of Jonny Arno's people. His PR person, a man named Edward Thompkins, called to warn us of deceitful behavior by trying to undercut the opening of Osteria Arno."

"Deceitful behavior? What's he talking about? The prix fixe dinner?"

"Yes, the dinner. He told us that we are deliberately competing with Jonny before the restaurant is officially open this weekend. He said that if we don't cease doing it, he will put us out of business with bad publicity."

"He can't do that, can he?" I asked, feeling queasy.

"He can lie about us," said Rhonda, "but those of us locals will know better. It's the other people who don't know us or the hotel who could be affected."

"Oh, my God! We can't let something like that happen! What exactly does he want us to do?"

"End the special Italian meal today. He thought it was outrageous that we'd do something like that to another restaurateur in the area," said Rhonda.

"Oh, come on! What's he doing about other Italian restaurants here in Sabal? Is he going after them too?"

Rhonda let out a snort. "I asked him that and he said we're special and the only real competition Jonny has. I told him there were several other excellent restaurants around."

"And?"

"And he said that he had information from a reliable local person that we're number one in the area." Rhonda sighed. "Guess who that local is?"

My lips thinned. "Brock Goodwin. How did you end the call?

Rhonda huffed, "I told him to eff off, that we're doing our business our way without any intention of harming anyone else."

"Maybe like Vaughn says, we need to go to the police with this information. It's just a threat, I know, but I want the local police to be aware of the situation." I was beginning to get scared.

"Listen, Annie, I grew up with tough guys like this. You can't let them see your weaknesses. We'll do the dinner tonight and then stop until things have settled down after the opening of Jonny's restaurant."

"Okay, because we can't be put in the position of defending a smear campaign," I said firmly.

"On a better note," said Rhonda. "I stopped off at Angie's before coming to work. With the help of a tutor, Sally Kate is doing better in school. And Evan is on the soccer team. And little Bella is happy in pre-school. All of that makes me unbelievably happy. I know you shouldn't worry about your kids and grandkids so much, but I can't help it sometimes."

"It's a mom thing," I said. "Even though we don't get to see enough of Vaughn's two children, we're interested in all the news and sometimes worry about them as much as those who are here in town."

"I knew you'd make me feel better," said Rhonda. "When

are you coming in?"

"I'm about ready to leave. When I get there, I'll tell you about who I met at the beach." I ended the call before Rhonda could pressure me into telling her now.

At the hotel, Rhonda and I met with Bernie to discuss the threat from Edward Thompkins and to ask him to meet with the police. Having our concerns come from Bernie would make it seem less confrontational than a fight between Jonny and Rhonda and me.

"C'mon, let's go for a walk on the beach," said Rhonda. "I'm spitting mad about being caught up in this battle with Jonny and I need to work off some steam."

"Me, too. We can't run our hotel if we're afraid that it's going to be ruined by someone else," I said.

We walked through the lobby, where people were gathering for their day. At the pool, sunbathers were already stretched out even though the gray clouds from earlier were slow to move on. The sun was due to come out later, but some couldn't wait to stake their claim on a chaise lounge chair.

We quickly discarded our sandals and headed for the water's edge. We stood quietly, letting our worries settle between us.

I turned to Rhonda. "Maybe we should send flowers to Osteria Arno for their grand opening. That would seem like the neighborly thing to do."

Rhonda made a face. "True. We've done it for others. But I didn't like the tone of voice Edward Thompkins used with me. Even though I lost my temper and told him to fuck off, I think we need to be careful. But I don't know about flowers."

Her cell phone rang. Rhonda checked it. "Speak of the devil." She answered the call.

I listened to the conversation and became startled when Rhonda said, "Okay, thank you. We'll let you know."

"What's that about?" I asked.

"We have been officially invited to a celebration at Osteria Arno tonight. Some of Jonny's backers and friends will be there. Seven o'clock. Our spouses are invited, too."

"That's a big change of attitude," I said. "But I think it's wise for us to be there. I'll call Vaughn and see if he wants to go with me. I'd certainly feel better if he was along."

"After all I've told Will about the situation, I'm sure he'll come," said Rhonda.

We walked toward the guesthouses. Being out on the property was a way for us to check on how the beach operations were going. What we called the sunset deck was open from mid-morning until nine at night. It had gone from a place to watch sunsets to a small food and drink operation where one could get refreshment throughout the day.

"Well, look who's getting some sun," said Rhonda as we approached Philippa and Harper on the beach in front of the guesthouses. The two of them were sitting on large beach towels.

"It's a surprise to see you out here," said Philippa.

"What are you doing?" Harper asked. "Taking a break?"

"Yes," I said. "It's the best way for us to talk privately and to relax."

Philippa patted the empty space next to her. "Please have a seat. If you're willing, I could use some advice."

I glanced at Rhonda.

"Okay," she said. "I'll sit. But I'll need help getting up."

"Deal," I said. Rhonda was in much better shape than she thought.

Rhonda and I sat down, and the girls formed a circle with us.

"Thanks," said Philippa. "I need some honest thoughts. Luciano and I aren't interested in marriage like our grandparents planned when we were children. I don't want to dishonor them, but they're old-fashioned and see this marriage as a way to keep the families together."

"And?" said Rhonda.

"And I'm in love with Chet. As crazy as it sounds, it's true. We met in New York over a year ago and had a wonderful time together for a magical night. We lost contact. Meeting him here at your hotel is like a gift from heaven. Especially when I'm getting pressure from my parents to settle down."

"How old are you?" I asked.

"Thirty-one," Philippa said. "Old enough that it's become a concern for my parents."

"Old enough to make your own decisions," said Rhonda. "As a mother myself, I'm concerned about my children's happiness. I can't believe your mother isn't, as well."

"We know how you feel about the circumstances," I said to Philippa. "What does Chet think?"

Philippa blushed. "He told me he loves me and wants to have a future together."

"Then, what's the problem?" asked Rhonda.

"It means that Luciano won't inherit his family's vineyard," said Philippa. "And I'm not certain that condition will change. It's all so mixed up. Luciano's younger brothers run the vineyard and are doing a superb job. Luciano doesn't have an interest in growing grapes but is interested in the business end of it. And now he's met Harper and wants to stay in Florida, like me."

"How does your mother feel about this?" I asked Philippa.

"She's very torn, unwilling to hurt family but wanting me to be happy," she answered.

"How does Luciano feel about all this?" asked Rhonda.

Philippa and Harper exchanged glances.

"Luciano and I are dating," said Harper. "It's too early to say what will happen, but he's fantastic."

"So, his losing the vineyard isn't an issue for him?" I asked.

Both girls shook their heads. "His younger brothers want it."

I studied the young, beautiful women and thought about what exciting lives lay ahead for them.

"My parents will say that everything is happening too fast," said Philippa. "How did you two know your husbands were right for you? I know you were married before you met the men you're married to now."

I turned to Rhonda.

She let out a little sigh. "I'm not going to lie. The minute I met Will I fell for him."

"I was witness to it," I said, recalling the way Will and Rhonda had simply stared at one another, their smiles wide.

"How about you, Ann?" Harper asked.

"I was intrigued by Vaughn but was so unsure of myself after my divorce. I couldn't believe he'd really be interested in me. He was still grieving the death of his wife, and he was a television star everyone loved."

"Yes, but Vaughn was attracted to you from the beginning even though he hesitated to act on it," said Rhonda supporting me.

"It's been a wonderful marriage," I said. "I still get those tingles."

"See? That's what I get with Chet," said Philippa. "I don't want to give those up."

I held up my hand. "I get it. I really do. And, personally, I agree. But I don't want your parents to think we've influenced you in any way. That's not what we're doing."

Philippa gave me a thoughtful look. "Thanks for letting me

air my problems. I've got a lot to think about."

We helped Rhonda to her feet and stood together for a moment.

"I love women being able to talk to one another," I said.

"It's all going to work out as long as you're honest about your feelings," said Rhonda. "I know what it's like growing up with parents you want to please."

"Is there anything we can do to help either of you while you're here?" I asked. "Harper and Philippa, I hope you'll continue working for us."

Rhonda looked away and frowned at two men walking toward us wearing business suits.

"I wonder what they want," she growled softly.

CHAPTER SEVENTEEN

WE MOVED AWAY FROM THE GIRLS AND MET THE strangers as they approached us.

"Hello. What are you doing here on the hotel's beach," I asked them.

One man, a little older and tougher looking, said, "I work for Jonny."

"And I work for Edward Thompkins," said the younger, more pleasant man with him. "We've been tasked with making sure you come to the private party at Osteria Arno tonight. My boss called you, but no definite answer was given. He feels it's important to be able to show the community mutual support between us."

"I see," I said, aware Rhonda was annoyed. "We'd already decided to attend. Is that satisfactory?"

"Yes," said the young man.

"Bring your husband with you," the older man said to me. "We always like stars at our events. The newspaper and local news station will be there."

Both men said goodbye, turned, and walked away.

"That's called bullying. I don't care how old we are, how successful we are at our jobs, we don't deserve to be treated like that," fumed Rhonda.

"That's called covering your ass," I said. "Their PR man must've realized what a mistake it was to attack us when we have so many friends in the area. Let him try to turn Jonny into an amiable, likeable guy. He won't get too far."

"It'll take more than an invitation to a party to make that

happen," said Rhonda.

I turned around. Philippa and Harper had picked up their things and gone inside.

"Guess I'd better go home and get ready for a party. I want to look my best," said Rhonda.

"Yes, it's going to be quite a show and will take a lot on our parts to pretend we care."

That evening, after gamely agreeing to accompany me, we walked to Vaughn's car, and he helped me inside. "Thanks," I told him. "I know you don't like these kinds of social events."

"For you, I'm happy to do it," Vaughn said, sliding behind the wheel. "Besides, I don't trust this Jonny character. There are too many indications that he is not the kind of man you need to be dealing with."

"I believe his PR rep is beginning to see that Jonny doesn't have the support of either the business community he left behind or the one he's trying to build here for his new restaurant. Bernie has been in touch with other restaurant owners on the coast, and they're not happy with Jonny's attitude either."

We drove in silence and arrived at Osteria Arno to see a stream of high-end cars waiting for the valets to take care of them.

Flashes of pink from specially mounted lights swept the front of the restaurant in continuing arcs.

Valets wearing white pants and shirts with Osteria Arno is bright pink letters took care of the car for us.

Vaughn took hold of my elbow and ushered me inside the restaurant. We were greeted by young girls offering glasses of champagne and wearing skimpy pink shorts and white, sleeveless blouses with Osteria Arno in sparkly pink letters.

I took a glass and moved along inside.

An older woman came over to us and began talking to Vaughn about his latest movie. I gazed around the room and saw Jonny talking to a group of men in dark business suits. He noticed me but didn't indicate it in any way.

I walked into the bar and found Helena Naylor, the mayor of Sabal, talking with a group of people. She saw me and waved me over.

"How are you, Ann? Dorothy Stern was looking for you. I think she moved into the dining room. She didn't look happy."

"Is Brock Goodwin here tonight?" I asked.

"Yes, he is. I believe he and Dorothy had an argument." Helena introduced me to the one man in the group I didn't know and then after speaking with him for a moment, I made my way into the dining room.

Dorothy Stern was sitting at one of the small tables set up around a cocktail buffet. Glass of champagne in hand, she was glaring at Brock, who was talking to two women standing nearby. I went right over to her.

She looked up at me. Behind the thick lenses of her glasses, her bright eyes shone. "I was hoping you'd be here. Brock is here, as well, and telling everyone that Jean-Luc is unable to cook at the restaurant anymore that you've hired some new, young chef."

I gritted my teeth. I'd have to ruin my evening and speak to him. Hopefully, before Rhonda got wind of this news. She wouldn't stop at a few F-bombs.

"Thanks for telling me," I said, and moved over to the small group with Brock.

"Evening, everyone."

"I'm sorry to hear about Jean-Luc," said one of the women. "I just love his food."

"Jean-Luc broke his ankle, but not too badly. He'll be back

at work very soon. Until then, he's running the kitchen from home."

The woman frowned and looked at Brock.

"I don't know what Brock has told you, but one must be careful about who's speaking," I said, forcing myself to smile.

Brock looked as if I'd slapped his face. "Well, I ..."

"Hello, everyone," said Rhonda joining us.

Brock excused himself, and I let out a sigh of relief.

We women chatted for a few moments, and then I led Rhonda aside to tell her what Dorothy had told me.

"That prick! Won't he ever stop?" Rhonda hissed.

"Oh, oh. Here comes Edward Thompkins. Let's play it cool," I said, forcing another pleasant look as we faced him.

"'Evening, ladies. I haven't officially introduced myself. Edward Thompkins. I'm delighted you could make it this evening. After all, we're neighbors, so to speak. I see you sent a beautiful floral arrangement for the occasion."

A tall thin man with sharp facial features, he oozed a fake friendliness I didn't trust.

"It's a very congenial neighborhood. We want it to stay that way," I said.

"Of course, of course," Edward said turning to Rhonda. "We were sorry to learn about Jean-Luc not being able to work for some time."

Rhonda gave him a puzzled look. "Who told you that? Your neighborhood informant?"

"Well, I thought ..." Edward began.

"He's going to be back in the kitchen later this week," I said. "In the meantime, we have a very competent staff, as you know."

"I didn't realize ..." Edward said and then gave us a bow. "I'm sorry. I need to talk to someone who just arrived."

He walked away, and Rhonda and I shook our heads as

Vaughn and Will walked over to us.

Vaughn leaned down and whispered in my ear, "The food isn't that good. Nothing exciting."

Terri Thomas from the newspaper joined us. "Do you mind if I have my photographer take a photo of the four of you?"

"Not at all," I said, getting approving nods from the other three.

As the photographer was arranging us, Jonny came over. "Mind if I break into the group?"

Terri's eyes widened, but she said, "Not a problem, please step in the middle."

Vaughn smoothly put his arm around me and drew me away from Jonny who's started to fling his arms around Rhonda and me.

We smiled and stood together for a couple of shots and then Jonny moved away without a word to us.

"He's as bad as you say, Rhonda," said Will shaking his head.

A group of men wearing dark slacks and dark shirts came in with women wearing fancy cocktail dresses and lots of jewelry. I assumed they were more of the backers for the restaurant.

One of the women noticed Vaughn and rushed over to him. "Vaughn Sanders! I'm one of your biggest fans!"

Rhonda and Will moved away.

I stayed to support Vaughn and was rewarded when the woman, Rosie Rossi, told us how her husband helped a lot of people in the restaurant business.

"How does that work?" I asked her.

She waved her hand in dismissal. "I don't get involved in all the details but in this case, Jonny Arno is a friend."

"Rosie!" a deep voice called.

Rosie jumped and said to Vaughn, "I've got to go. But

before I do, can I take a selfie with you?"

For an instant Vaughn hesitated, then gamely allowed her to take the photo.

After she left, I took Vaughn's arm. "We can leave anytime. I've met Jonny's PR person and you've met Jonny."

"Thanks. I'm ready," said Vaughn.

We went to find Rhonda and Will but realized they'd already left.

Outside, while we waited for the valet to come with Vaughn's car, we heard someone say, "This food can't compare to The Beach House Hotel's restaurant. Their Italian special was absolutely delicious."

Edward came out of the restaurant, saw us, and came over. "I hope you're not leaving. The best is yet to come. We're opening a chocolate fountain, a much smaller version similar to the one at the Bellagio in Vegas."

Hunting for an excuse, I turned to Vaughn.

"Sorry. I have an engagement," he said politely. "But I'm sure we'll see it when we return for a meal after your official opening."

Edward ran his fingers through his hair and gave us an apologetic look. "It was decent of you to come. I know it was a last-minute invitation."

"Thank you," I said sincerely. He was obviously a man under a lot of stress and just might be beginning to realize his client was more difficult than he'd thought.

On the way home from the party, Vaughn was quiet.

"What's wrong?" I asked.

"I know we've discussed it before, but I don't trust that man or the people supporting him."

I sighed. "We're just going to have to deal with him."

"You're right. But I don't like it," said Vaughn.

We arrived home, and Vaughn and I decided to take a dip in our heated pool. It was a pleasant night and both of us were a little tense after attending Jonny's reception.

We checked on Robbie and found him sprawled across his bed sound asleep.

"I swear it's one of his growing days," I whispered. "Look how tall he is spread out like that."

Vaughn put an arm around me. "Our boy is growing fast."

Cindy eyed us from where she lay next to Robbie.

We patted her and left to go to our bedroom.

Vaughn took off his shirt. "I don't know about you, I think it's a perfect night for a skinny dip."

"Sounds fine with me," I said. We had total privacy in the pool, and I loved the freedom it gave us.

A few minutes later, we were enjoying the refreshing water and loosening our tight muscles by floating on our backs and gazing up at the stars.

"I always feel as if our troubles disappear when I see the stars and realize what a small part I play in the context of things," I said.

"*You* make my troubles disappear," said Vaughn tugging me to him and wrapping his arms around me.

When our lips met, it seemed as if the stars were shining just for us.

CHAPTER EIGHTEEN

WHEN I DID MY USUAL MORNING WALK AT THE HOTEL'S beach, I saw Philippa emerge from the guesthouse with her mother.

Surprised, I hesitated and then moved ahead to greet them. I hoped Philippa's mother would be understanding about the situation that had unfolded between Luciano and her daughter.

Philippa hurried ahead. "Morning, Ann. Heads up. My parents don't know anything about Chet and me and Luc and Harper. Please don't say anything. I haven't had a chance to talk to my mother."

"I understand," I said, smiling as I approached Catarina Ferrera. "Lovely day. When did you get back?"

"Late last night. I wanted to return as soon as possible because I was unaware my husband had sent for Luciano to come to Florida."

"I've met him. He's a very pleasant young man." Observing Philippa's worried look, I quickly changed the subject. "By the way, while you were gone, Philippa did some consulting work in the kitchen for our chef, Chet. It helped us out of a difficult position when our master chef hurt his ankle and couldn't come in. And now she's agreed to work in our hospitality department."

Catarina smiled. "Philippa mentioned that to me. She says she loves it here in Florida working at the hotel. It's satisfying to see her so enthusiastic about something."

"Any luck with the housing hunt? I asked her.

"My real estate agent says he's found the perfect house for us. I'm to take a look at it sometime this morning. I'm delighted to be able to spend part of the year in Sabal, and with Philippa so happy here, having a house is important to me."

"I wish you luck with it," I said. "I'm going to head back, but I'm glad I had the opportunity to see you. As always, if you need anything during your stay, please let us know."

I turned and headed toward the hotel for another busy day.

When I told Rhonda that Catarina was back at the hotel, she agreed with me that it was best for us to stay out of the way and carry on with our business.

Over the next days, we met with the hospitality department and made sure all knew what their roles were. A meeting with our daughters and Harper went well, and aside from listening to their ideas, Rhonda and I left it in their hands.

"Wow! Having our girls and now, Harper and Philippa, working on projects makes me realize how lovely it would be if we could semi-retire," said Rhonda one afternoon.

"I don't want to jinx anything, but I like the idea myself," I said. "While it's quiet, why don't you and Will take that short getaway you wanted?"

"Really? I'd love it. Just a three-day weekend will be great," Rhonda said, lifting her cellphone. "I'm going to call Will right now."

I got up and left her to her discussion with Will. I wanted to see how Jean-Luc was doing directing his staff. He was wearing a soft cast and though he couldn't walk on his foot yet, he was able to move around using a freedom leg brace, which took the weight off his injured ankle.

As happy as he was to be back at work, he was able to work

for only a few hours in the afternoon and a few more in the evening. Rhonda and I had noticed that the more time Jean-Luc was able to spend with his staff, the happier they and he were.

"Hi," I said, walking into his office. "How are things going?"

"Okay," he said. "Chet and Ricardo are a great team for me."

"I'm glad to hear it. I just wanted to warn you that with another wedding this weekend, we'll be busy. And Rhonda might not be here, so I need to make sure you're able to handle the wedding dinner and post-wedding breakfast along with everything else."

"*Oui,*" he said so quickly I decided not to press the issue. Like all chefs, Jean-Luc had an ego, and I didn't want to bruise it.

"Okay, thanks. That's all I needed," I said.

I returned to the office to find Rhonda on the phone with Angie. "Yes, we'll be gone for three nights, four days," she told her. "Thanks. Just wanted you to know." She looked up at me and winked. "Ann will hold down the fort for us."

After ending the call, Rhonda rose and did a little dance behind her chair. "This is exactly what I need. Are you sure you don't mind?"

"Not at all. When Vaughn finishes an assignment, he likes to spend time at home. He says it grounds him. I'm just happy it's working out for you and Will to get away. It's been a while since you've been able to do it."

"You're telling me," Rhonda joked. "Time for me to wear a sexy nightgown and get some action."

I laughed. Theirs was a happy marriage, but I knew from experience that with kids in the house, there wasn't always the opportunity for what she called "action".

"I just spoke to Jean-Luc. I'm comfortable that the kitchen is ready to handle the wedding. Now, I want to make sure Lorraine's crew is ready, too."

"I'll go with you. I need to know there will be no trouble while I'm gone," said Rhonda. She wrapped her arm around me for a quick hug. "You're such a sweetheart to let me go."

In Lorraine's office, her assistant, Lauren, was going over protocol for wedding arrivals with Philippa.

They looked up when we entered.

"I'm glad to see you working together for the upcoming wedding," I said. "It's a small one, so should be easier than some. But no matter the size, we want to give our wedding parties the best experience we can."

"Who knows? You might be planning your own wedding here one day," Rhonda said to them.

I rolled my eyes, and everyone laughed.

"Seriously," said Rhonda. "We do an excellent wedding business because we show that we care. Every detail is important."

"True," said Lauren. "That's why we've developed all these tracking sheets."

"Where's Lorraine?" I asked.

"She went to a meeting, but she'll be back a little later," said Lauren. "She's booked herself to handle the wedding this weekend."

"That means you, Philippa, will work with an assortment of people." I glanced at Rhonda. "See? Everything is all set in this department."

"Will and I are going away for a few days, and I wanted to be sure I wasn't leaving at a bad time," explained Rhonda. "Thanks so much for your help."

"See you later," I said.

Walking back to our office, Rhonda said, "I'm going to go home to make sure things are settled there. I'll check in with you in the morning before we take off."

"Okay, but you don't need to. Just relax and enjoy some time off. Vaughn and I will get our chance later."

Rhonda gave me a long hug. "I knew you and I would be the best partners ever."

Laughing, I said, "Go. Have a delightful time. We'll be fine."

The next day, I stood alone at the top of the stairs waiting to greet the bride and her family. The space beside me felt empty but I was delighted that Rhonda had called with the news that the small resort where they were staying was beautiful and relaxing.

A white limousine pulled up to the front of the hotel and I drew a deep breath, hoping this weekend would go well. Lorraine had told me that Virginia "Ginny" Collington was very refined and expected the best for her daughter. Her husband, a CEO of a tech company, was well-traveled and had heard of The Beach House Hotel through a senator friend.

The limo pulled to a stop and the driver raced around the car to open the back passenger door.

A striking woman wearing her blonde hair in a sleek bun stepped out of the car in a pale blue linen suit. A string of pearls sat atop a white silk blouse. Matching pearl earrings sat in her ear lobes.

A gray-haired man dressed in a tan summer suit followed her.

They stood aside while their daughter exited the limo. Trim like her mother, she had an angelic, pink-cheeked face framed by honey-colored hair. Sparkling blue eyes met mine as I said, "Welcome to The Beach House Hotel."

"We're very pleased to be here," said Virginia. "This is my husband Clark Collington and my daughter, Audrey."

"We've heard great things about the hotel," said Clark, shaking my hand. "Nothing's too good for my little girl."

"Daddy," groaned Audrey, smiling at him and then turning to me. "This wedding is really hard on him."

"I do gain a son," he said grinning.

"Nate and his family are arriving a little later," said Virginia. "We were able to fly in a private jet thanks to one of Clark's friends who was doing business in Florida."

"Let me walk you inside," I said. "The bags will be taken care of for you."

I held my head high as I led them up the stairs and into the lobby of the hotel. I remembered my first sight of the living room that had been turned into a lobby and how impressed I'd been. I still thought it was beautiful and welcoming.

"Oh," said Virginia. "It's as lovely as its photographs."

Bernie walked across the lobby to greet them.

I said goodbye to the family and left it to the staff to take care of them. I loved small, upscale weddings like this one with only forty guests to pamper.

An hour or so later, I was called to greet the groom's family.

As their limousine pulled up to the front of the hotel, I went down the stairs to greet them.

The driver helped an older woman wearing slacks and a knit top out of the car. Smiling, the woman brushed back gray curls and waited for her son to climb out of the back seat.

Tall and broad-shouldered, a young man with straight, brown hair emerged wearing jeans and a Boston Red Sox T-shirt.

His father came around the car and I saw how closely the

two men resembled one another.

"Welcome to The Beach House Hotel," I said. "We're so happy you're here."

"I'm Bud Bradbury and this is my wife, Abby, and my son, the groom, Nate."

"I think you've got a perfect weekend for the wedding. No storms," I said as I led them up the front steps and into the lobby.

"Nate!" Audrey cried, running across the lobby to greet him.

He swept her off her feet and into his arms as if she weighed nothing, and I realized he must have been active in sports.

His parents laughed as Nate swung Audrey around before setting her down in front of them.

Nate's mother hugged Audrey, and they stood aside while his father registered them at the front desk.

"Where are you having the Rehearsal Dinner?" I asked. "I know it's not here at the hotel."

"We thought we'd decided to go to a French restaurant in town but then we got a special invitation from Osteria Arno to have our dinner there," said Abby.

"Really?" I asked, wondering how Osteria Arno had gotten the names of our wedding group.

"They gave us an excellent price and said since they were new in the area we'd get special service," said Abby. "They even offered a post-wedding brunch. I told them they'd have to contact the bride's parents for that."

"I see." I worked hard not to give away my frustration at Osteria Arno's attempt to poach my guests.

Bernie arrived to greet the family and I said quietly, "We need to talk."

I went to my office to consider what, if anything, we should do about the situation. I called the wedding planning office to see if the wedding breakfast was still on.

"Yes," said Lauren. "Everything is in place."

"Let me know right away if there are any problems."

Bernie knocked on my door and opened it. "You wanted to see me?"

"Yes," I said, waving him inside.

He took a seat, and I filled him in on the conversation I'd had with the groom's mother.

Bernie shook his head. "It undermines the way we in the state restaurant association have agreed to cooperate. I'll try to get to the bottom of this and get back to you."

"How do you think they got the information about the groom's family?" I asked. "Do you think someone here at the hotel is cooperating with them at Osteria Arno?"

"There are ways for them to find out, but we'll want to check on that too," said Bernie. "It happens."

CHAPTER NINETEEN

THE NEXT MORNING, I DECIDED TO TAKE MY WALK ON the beach before the activities of the hotel prevented me from doing so. I'd spent a restless night worrying about the wedding, wondering how the rehearsal dinner had gone at Osteria Arno. In the years since Rhonda and I opened the hotel, we'd never had any problems with any other hospitality members in business. But I couldn't shake the feeling that this wedding was a test of how things would be going forward with Jonny and his crew.

Catarina saw me and waved.

I waved back and went to meet her.

"What a beautiful day," I said. "I'm glad to see you out here enjoying it."

"It's a beautiful place to think," she said smiling at me.

"For me, too. How did it go with the house you viewed?" I asked.

Catarina's eyes lit with pleasure. "I've put a bid on the house the agent thought I'd like. It's perfect. It's in Rhonda's neighborhood. Just a couple of doors down."

"I'm so happy for you," I gushed. "You'll be lucky to get it. It's a sought-after location."

"The real estate agent assures me I've got it, but until I sign on the dotted line, I won't relax."

"Where's Philippa? I thought she might be walking with you," I said.

"She's already at the hotel working on the wedding arrangements. I've never seen her so happy." Catarina sighed.

"We still have to convince her father that she and Luciano are making the right decision to turn away from an old-fashioned family promise. She says she's in love with Chet, but I don't see how that could happen so quickly."

"Rhonda and I were able to talk to her and Harper about things, and Philippa told us she feels very strongly about her relationship with Chet. After meeting, they've never forgotten one another. I have a daughter the same age, and I have the impression that Philippa was very sincere."

"She tells me she tried to find out where Chet went when he left New York," said Catarina. "She's always been a headstrong girl."

"Better that than not knowing what she wants," I said.

Catarina settled her gaze on me, hesitated, and then said, "You're right. I should remember that. I just want her to be happy. And Chet seems like a nice young man. Thanks for listening. Now I'll need to make my husband understand Philippa's decision not to marry Luciano, who's a very suitable man for her."

"I never had a normal family growing up, so I don't know what to say that might be helpful."

Catarina chuckled. "Even after living with Enrico for almost thirty-five years, I don't either."

"Remember, if you need anything, please let me know."

She gave me a quick hug. "You've been a big help. Thanks."

Still smiling, I went on my way.

Back at the hotel, I inspected the library where the wedding was going to take place. I found Lauren and Philippa talking to Danielle from Tropical Fleurs.

"Hello, how's it going?" I asked them.

Danielle gripped her hands together. "I don't know how it

happened, but the Collington order for flowers got mixed up with an order for Osteria Arno and I've run out of pink roses for the wedding ceremony and the dinner following it."

My heart sank at the news. Was this another problem with Jonny? "How specific was the order? Did it include other flowers?"

"Yes, but we had planned on using mostly roses," said Danielle.

"How about using hydrangeas, calla lilies, and snapdragons? To me, that's lovelier than roses. Let's call Audrey and see what she thinks. Pull together some pictures of flowers to show her."

Danielle messaged her photos of a variety of flowers and then called Audrey.

After discussing the photos and explaining the type of bouquets and baskets of flowers they could use, Danielle gave a thumbs up to Ann. "I think you'll be pleased," Danielle told Audrey and her mother. "And, of course, there will be no extra charge for the change in flowers."

When the call ended, Danielle let out a sigh of relief. "I'm so glad Audrey and her mother are understanding people. But I'm mad as hell that this happened. We also had a problem with flowers for the rehearsal dinner at Osteria Arno. Ann, you know how reliable we are."

"Indeed, I do," I said. "I think the problem is with the restaurant. Not you."

"Thanks for your support," said Danielle. "I'll hurry back to the shop and deliver the flowers on time."

"Does something like this happen very often?" Philippa asked me after Danielle left.

"Weddings can be one crisis after another. But no, Danielle and Tropical Fleurs never give us cause for alarm. I can't help but wonder if this has anything to do with Jonny trying to harass us."

"We'll make sure to be doubly careful with the rest of the preparations," said Lauren. "A crew from housekeeping is coming to place coverings and bows on the chairs."

"Thanks for your help," I said and left to go talk to Bernie. He wanted to be informed of any problems with Osteria Arno and Jonny so he could keep an accurate record.

When I reached Bernie's office, he waved me inside.

"How are things going?" he asked me.

"Pretty well, but there's something I need to talk to you about," I said, and gave him the details of the problem with the flowers. "I can't help wondering if someone from Jonny's team did this on purpose as another way to cause us problems."

"It could be," said Bernie. "I discovered that the owner of one of the limousine companies we use has supplied information to Jonny's people regarding guests who were coming here to the hotel to talk about wedding plans. That's how the groom's family for the Collington wedding was given their deal at Osteria Arno for the rehearsal dinner."

"What are we going to do about that?" I asked.

"The only thing we can do is suggest that our guests use a different limousine company for their travel," said Bernie. "I will also send a letter to the state hotel association to warn them of such activity."

"Guess that's all we can do," I said, unable to hold back a sigh. "I wish we didn't have to deal with issues like this."

"There should be no reason to do so. In all my years of working, I've never had to deal with such petty stuff," said Bernie. "But I think Jonny is a man under siege. He's been warned that he must make the restaurant succeed. Apparently, he's being backed by some unforgiving people."

A look of understanding passed between us.

I left his office feeling discouraged and decided to take another walk on the beach.

Outside, I breathed in the fresh salty air and felt my body loosen. The hotel business wasn't easy at its best, but I'd never felt so insecure about it. We couldn't let someone's jealousy ruin our business or make running the hotel more difficult than it was.

As I walked onto the sand, I heard someone call my name and turned to see Abby Bradbury, the mother of the groom, waving at me.

She came over to me. "Such a lovely morning for our wedding day."

"How was the rehearsal dinner a Osteria Arno?" I asked.

Abby shook her head. "Not great. There was apparently a fight in the kitchen and our food arrived late and some of it was cold. The flavors and all were fine, but the service was terrible. My husband is an impatient man, but the rest of us were upset too."

"I'm sorry that happened to you," I said. "There are other excellent restaurants in the area who could've hosted your event."

"I can't wait to have dinner here at the hotel. I've heard nothing but nice things about your restaurant," Abby said.

"I think you'll be pleased," I said. "Enjoy your stay."

Abby left and I headed to the water to feel the soothing waves at my ankles. I was glad Rhonda was away, hopefully relaxing. My stress level was high. Hers would've been ready to explode if she knew what was happening.

That afternoon, I arrived for the wedding just after four o'clock to make sure everything was ready for the ceremony which would be held at five in the library.

Philippa, Lauren, and Lorraine were in the library making last minute adjustments to the chairs which had been formed into a semi-circle around the altar where the minister, bride, and groom would stand.

"It looks lovely," I said admiring the pink bows sitting atop each chair back covered in white cloth. Looking closer, I noticed that each bow held a tiny sprig of white stock flowers.

"The bride's bouquet is stunning," said Philippa.

"And you should see the floral arrangements Danielle made for the dining room," Lauren said. "I love this part of planning a wedding and seeing how it all comes together."

"It's all in the details," said Lorraine. "Now, you can go get ready to usher people from the lobby to here in the library. They will find their own seats except for the four designated for the bride and groom's parents."

The minister, Margaret Chase, arrived with a young guitar player. She was accustomed to overseeing weddings at the hotel and stood aside as the musician set up and started playing music.

"I think you'll enjoy this group," I said to her. "Everyone is very pleasant."

"That makes my job easier," said Margaret. "Facing a couple about to be married gives me insight into how long I think the union will last." Margaret was a middle-aged woman who was a mother of five and knew when someone was not being truthful.

After checking the dining room, I went back to the site of the wedding. Rhonda and I tried to attend as many weddings at the hotel as we could. It was always interesting.

The music continued as people walked in and took their seats. The groom and his brother, the best man, stood in front of the group.

After three of the parents were seated, a pretty woman

walked in wearing a stunning pink dress and holding a sweet bouquet. She stood by the minister and then the music changed to Ed Sheeran's "Thinking Out Loud."

Audrey appeared holding onto her father's arm. The simple white sleeveless dress embraced her torso and then fell in silky folds to her ankles. She wore a tiny tiara of flowers in her hair, and I had the feeling once again of sensing an angelic person. Her blue eyes were lit with excitement and the look of love she sent Nate had his eyes watering along with those of us in the audience.

Pleasantly surprised by the simple elegance of the wedding, I left the room to check in with Lorraine before leaving the hotel to go home,

CHAPTER TWENTY

VAUGHN MET ME AT THE DOOR WHEN I ARRIVED HOME. "Good evening, Mrs. Sanders. May I interest you in a dinner date at your favorite French restaurant?"

"That sounds delicious. What about Robbie?"

"He's already consumed two hamburgers and fries and coleslaw at his favorite place," said Vaughn chuckling. "Now, he's next door playing video games with Brett."

"Perfect," I said. "I really need a break. It's been tough having Rhonda gone for a couple of days." As I said the words, I realized how true it was. She was a business partner in every sense. Being able to talk through situations with her relieved a lot of stress. I was the worrier; she was the comforter.

"Come here." Vaughn pulled me into his arms and wrapped me in them. "Sounds like this is the right evening to fuss over you. I'm glad I'm here to do it. I heard from my agent, and he wants me to film a commercial in the Rocky Mountains sometime next week. It shouldn't take long, but I'll be away for a few days."

"Then I'm very glad we have this time together. When are our dinner reservations?"

"Any time after I've had a chance to have you to myself. Margot at *André's* is holding a table for us."

"Oh, perfect," I said, lifting my face for a much-needed kiss.

André's was tucked into a small alleyway downtown. The owners, Margot and André Durand, were friends of Jean-

Luc's and were supporters of ours.

After we were seated, Vaughn and I shared a bottle of wine.

The aroma of butter and garlic filled the air and my nostrils as I gazed at the menu. Making love with Vaughn had helped to settle my nerves, but I still had to get through the wedding breakfast tomorrow before I could relax.

Margot came over to us. "Have you decided what you want?"

"I'm going to have the *ratatouille*," I said.

"Excellent. We had delivery of some fresh vegetables especially for it."

"Is your *coq au vin* as delicious as always?" Vaughn said to her, grinning.

"When we heard you were in town, André and I made sure of it," said Margo, chuckling. It had become a joke that no matter what else was on the menu, Vaughn ordered coq au vin.

Margot left, and Vaughn sat back in his chair and studied me. "It's nice to see you smile. I wish there was something I could do to help you deal with Jonny Arno."

"Me, too. But things are bound to settle down," I said. "Have you heard from Nell lately? I talked to her last week, and they're still planning on coming for Thanksgiving."

"I called her this morning," he said. "She, Clint, and the kids are fine. They aren't quite ready to move to Florida but someday they will be."

"I would love it," I said.

"So, would I," he said. "It makes me happy that you and she are close. I think you and Ellie would have been friends if you'd ever had the chance to meet." Vaughn and Ellie had been happily married before she died of cancer.

We discussed his son, Ty, and his family, and then we moved on to Vaughn's latest project. It was such a relief to talk about anything but the hotel.

Our meal came, and as I tasted my vegetable stew, I couldn't help emitting a little groan of pleasure.

Vaughn chuckled and took a bit of his chicken dish. "M-m-m, so good."

The restaurant was emptying of people when André came from the kitchen and pulled up a chair to our table. "*Bonsoir* to two of my favorite people. Now that you're about finished with your meal, I wanted to speak to you about some things I've been hearing."

Vaughn and I exchanged glances.

"Is this about Jonny Arno?" I asked him.

He made a face and nodded. "He's in trouble. I heard he borrowed a lot of money from the mafia to open his restaurant, and now he can't pay it back. They overspent on the construction and the décor, and Jonny bought that fancy car of his. I don't think that restaurant will be open much longer."

"I've wondered about it," I admitted.

"Two members of the kitchen staff have come to me for work, which I couldn't give them," said André. "I think they, too, suspect a bad ending."

André stood and a waitress cleared our table.

Margot appeared carrying a plate of Macarons. "Here's a little sweet for your dessert. Enjoy!"

I reached for the meringue-based confection and took a bite.

Vaughn did the same, grinning when we both said, "M-m-m" at the same time.

When it was time for us to leave, we thanked Andre and Margot for a delicious meal and then decided to walk around town to work off some of our dinner.

Walking hand in hand, gazing into the windows of stores

now closed, I felt as if all was right with the world. Sabal was a charming town on Florida's Gulf Coast, and I felt lucky to be able to call it home. After living most of my life in Boston, I'd loved coming to a warm, more tropical climate. Even now, watching the fronds of the palm trees sway in the breeze, I couldn't help my pleasure.

Vaughn gave my hand a squeeze and I impulsively stopped and threw my arms around him.

"Well, what do we have here?" I heard a familiar voice say and froze.

I turned to face Brock Goodwin. "What are you doing in town?"

"I could ask Vaughn the same question," he said. "In between movies?"

"For a bit," said Vaughn, keeping a hand on my shoulder.

"How are things going at the restaurant?" I asked him.

"As well as can be expected for a restaurant of this caliber. It's really beautiful. As you know, I helped the interior decorator by providing some of the décor items from my import business. It's worked out rather well."

I could feel Vaughn's fingers squeeze my shoulder and knew that he, as well as I, was trying not to react.

"See you around," I managed to say and watched Brock walk away with an added strut to his pace.

Chuckling softly, Vaughn and I continued our stroll.

The next morning, I slept in, cuddling Vaughn, knowing he'd be gone in a couple of days. His schedule had caused some problems and disappointments, but we managed to work with it. Having the hotel to run kept me busy along with family responsibilities. That helped.

Cindy nosed our bedroom door wider and then whined for

us to pick her up.

Vaughn lowered his torso out of bed, grabbed hold of her, and tossed her on the bed.

After licking us happily, she settled between us. There had been days when Robbie was little that he'd be there too. Now, as a young teenager, he was in his own bed asleep.

Reluctantly, I got up to shower and dress for the bridal breakfast. We did a great job of providing both a hearty breakfast and healthy snacks for wedding guests who were leaving to go home.

As I drove to the hotel, I was anxious to see if Philippa would be there to help Lorraine. Being responsive to the demands of others grew tiresome if you weren't really happy about doing it and following through. This would be an interesting test for her.

I went past the gates of the hotel and drove behind it to my usual parking space near the loading dock. Beside the dock, on an area reserved for staff breaks, I noticed Philippa and Chet kissing and couldn't hold back a smile. They were an adorable couple.

I got out of the car and headed inside, stopping to say hello to them before going to check on preparations for the wedding breakfast buffet.

Philippa caught up to me. "Morning, Ann. I want you to know I was just taking a break. I'm heading back to the dining room now."

"No problem, Philippa, as long as it doesn't interfere with work for the hotel by either you or Chet. How do you like working in the hospitality department?"

"I love it. I'm used to helping at receptions put on by my parents, and this is a lot more fun."

"Sometime next week, Rhonda and I will sit down with you to discuss a permanent plan for you."

"Thanks. My father is going to come down to Sabal in a few days to look at the house my mother wants to buy. I want him to know how serious I am about living and working here."

I gave her an encouraging smile. "Glad to hear it. How is Luciano doing?"

"He and Harper are getting along nicely. The truth is, Luc and I are relieved to be able to move along with our lives. I don't know how long he'll be staying here."

"Does his family know there will be no wedding between you and him?"

Philippa made a face and shrugged her shoulders. "I don't know. Luc is waiting to speak to my father."

We entered the dining room together.

"Hello," I said to Lauren who was adjusting the floral centerpiece on a small table holding dishes and silverware.

"'Morning," said Lauren. "Thanks, Philippa, for retrieving the flowers from last night's dinner."

"You're welcome. I would hate to see them go to waste," Philippa said.

"Have you coordinated timing with the kitchen?" I asked them.

A pretty blush crept up Philippa's cheek. "That's what I'd been doing when you saw me."

"Okay, fine," I said. "I'll be in my office if you need me."

I left and stopped in the kitchen to see what was happening there.

Consuela beamed at me as she pulled cinnamon rolls out of the oven. "*Buenos Dias.*"

"A quiet morning to be here," I said, grabbing a cup of coffee. "Thanks."

"When is Rhonda coming back?" she asked me, placing a

sweet roll on a plate and handing it to me.

"Late tomorrow night. It'll be great to have her back."

"The two of you together. That's what makes a great team," Consuela said. "It's always been that way."

I went to my office to work on a financial reconciliation of wedding expenses. Costs had to be carefully controlled for these events. This wedding was small and well-planned. But costs for larger ones often got out of control if their contracts didn't include everything.

I was reviewing numbers when there was a knock on the door and Harper came inside.

"Have a minute?" she asked.

"Sure. Have a seat," I said, seeing distress on her face. "What's going on?"

She leaned forward. "I want to be totally upfront with you. Luciano is asking me to travel to Italy to meet his family. He wants to see where our relationship might go. I told him about my commitment to you and Rhonda and that I'd need time to think about it."

"How do you feel about him? Isn't this very sudden?" I asked her.

"I'm falling for him hard. He's a bright, kind, gentle man whom I'm very attracted to."

"But?" I asked her.

"It might mean a whole different life if I go with him. I don't know that much about his family, and he hasn't met mine."

"How soon is he returning to Italy?" I asked.

"That's open. The vineyard is past the pressing period for the grapes so there's some flexibility. But I know I promised you and Rhonda that I'd work for you, and I don't want to go back on my word. That's important to me. I've drawn up a list of ideas for the bar, but I might not be able to implement them."

I studied her. "Do you think you love him, or do you know deep in your gut that you do? Enough to go to Italy and live a life there? That's a very big step. Why is he in such a hurry?"

Harper gave me a steady look. "He and Philippa are under a lot of pressure to follow through on an old family promise neither wants to keep. I know he's not a player and he'd never hurt me. He tells me he's never felt this way about any other woman. We've both been with other people, so I understand. I've never felt this way about any other man."

"As far as your word to Rhonda and me, we'll understand if you decide to go to Italy with him." My mind spun with an idea. "Are you both free this afternoon to go for a sail on my husband's boat. It's a great day for a sailing picnic."

Smiling, Harper said, "I think Luc would love it. I know I would."

"Great. Why don't you two come to my house at around two o'clock? "

Harper stood. "Thank you. I want to know what you think about Luc and me together. This will help."

"Exactly," I said smiling at her. "See you then."

She left and I called Vaughn to make those arrangements with him.

Upon hearing what I had in mind, he laughed. "It's true. There's nothing like being on a boat to expose the true nature of others."

CHAPTER TWENTY-ONE

HARPER AND LUCIANO ARRIVED AT MY HOUSE PROMPTLY at two o'clock.

Cindy and I went to the door to greet them. "Welcome! This is our Dachshund, Cindy. She'll be going out on the boat with us, too."

Both Harper and Luciano bent down to pet Cindy and then Harper handed me a bakery box. "Homemade canapés for the boat trip."

"Perfect. Thanks so much. Are you ready to head down to the boat?"

We walked down the slope of lawn to the dock where Vaughn and Robbie were waiting for us.

"We're all set as soon as Cindy is put in her life vest," said Vaughn.

I introduced him to Harper and Luciano and introduced Robbie.

Robbie took the box from me and went below to stow the goodies for later. Then he came up to the deck and took the wheel while everyone but Vaughn got settled in the cockpit. As captain, Vaughn explained the rules of sailing and how one must follow a captain's orders at all times, especially when the boat was coming about.

"Robbie, you start the engine and take the wheel while I cast off," said Vaughn.

With obvious pride, Robbie did as he was told.

Cindy settled between Harper and Luciano loving the attention they gave her.

Moments later, the boat eased from the dock and motored slowly out of the lagoon, past condos on the waterway, and out into the open Gulf.

Robbie and Vaughn worked in tandem to get the sails raised. As the wind filled the sails, Vaughn said, "Okay, cut the engine."

"I always love this moment," I said to Harper and Luciano. "It's such a special feeling to have it go quiet and listen to the soft sound of the boat moving through the water."

"*Sì*," said Luciano. "Thank you for including us." He glanced at Harper and then looked ahead.

"Do you and your family sail often?" Harper asked me.

"When Vaughn is home, it's an excellent way to relax and bring the family together again. My daughter, Liz, and her husband go sailing with us sometimes. And we're starting to get their triplets used to it."

"Your daughter has triplets?" Luciano asked, putting his arm around Harper.

I couldn't hold back a chuckle. "It's quite an experience."

"I come from a big family," said Luciano. "But no triplets."

We all laughed when he pretended to wipe his brow with relief.

"I think it's a good way to have children. Close together," Harper said.

Luciano gave her an approving look. "You could handle it."

They smiled at one another, their gazes lingering on each other.

After we'd sailed for a while and tacked a couple of times, Vaughn suggested we find a quiet spot, toss the anchor, and enjoy our appetizers and wine.

"Over there," said Robbie pointing to a cove along the shore.

"Okay, come about," said Vaughn just as Harper stood to

go below.

She was on the boat for a minute, and in the next one, she'd been swept into the water by the swinging boom.

I immediately grabbed a floating cushion and tossed it to her, hitting the back of Luciano as he swiftly dove into the water.

Robbie started the engine and helped Vaughn take down the sails.

As part of my training, I kept a steady eye on Harper and Luciano clinging together in the water, relieved to see the waves weren't an issue. It was clear that Luciano was an excellent swimmer.

Vaughn took over the wheel and guided the boat back alongside the swimmers.

Robbie tossed a rope ladder to them.

Harper grabbed it and began to climb up onto the deck.

When she was safe, Luciano swam to the end of the ladder and followed her up to the deck.

I checked Harper for any injuries and though she had a slight bruise on her shoulder, she told us she was fine. "I just feel foolish."

"No," said Vaughn. "I didn't see you get to your feet. So, the fault is mine."

"Thank God, you weren't seriously hurt," I said. "And Luciano, you were splendid. What a hero you are."

He shook his head. "It wasn't even a conscious decision. I just knew I wasn't going to let anything happen to Harper."

"Great job," said Vaughn clapping a hand on his shoulder. "I say it's time to have some refreshments."

I handed Harper and Luciano several beach towels. "Dry yourself off and keep yourselves warm. The wine will help."

They wrapped themselves in the towels and sat. Then Luciano pulled Harper to his side to keep her warm. "You okay?" he asked softly, stroking her back.

Harper nodded. "Thanks. You really are my hero."

He kissed her on the cheek and drew her closer.

We motored to the cove and anchored the boat. The evening was pleasant with warm temperatures and a dying wind that allowed us to be comfortable as we ate and drank and got to know one another better.

I noticed how kind Harper and Luciano were to Cindy and Robbie. As a mother, it meant a lot to me. And I watched the interaction between Harper and Luciano, noting how they couldn't keep their eyes off one another and how frequently they briefly touched hands.

The sun was going down as we motored back home, and a quiet peacefulness filled the boat. Regardless of the accident, it had been a wonderful sail. A meaningful one.

Later, when Vaughn and I talked privately about them, we agreed that Harper and Luciano showed all the signs of being a successful couple.

"Rhonda is going to be thrilled. Of course, she'll say it's because she knew it first and wanted it to happen."

Vaughn chuckled. "Rhonda is Rhonda, and we love her."

The next morning, Vaughn agreed to see Robbie off to school, and I wanted a quiet time on the beach to consider the week ahead.

The morning air was full of moisture, and I had the impression that the weather news might be right about the storm system developing off the coast of Africa. It was hurricane season, after all. I pulled my car through the gates of the hotel and noticed Chet and Philippa emerging from the apartment we'd given to Chet. It made me wonder if Harper and Luciano were sleeping there too.

I continued to my parking space behind the hotel. There, I tossed my sandals into the car and headed out to the beach, looking forward to some peaceful moments.

As usual, at this time of early morning, a quiet busyness hung over the area as people either jogged or walked along the beach and others stooped to collect shells. The cries of the seagulls and terns above me seemed even softer as if they too were not quite ready for the day to begin.

I sighed with pleasure and stepped into the water feeling as if I was part of both the present and the past. The waves rolled in and pulled away in a timeless fashion that never failed to make me grateful for such constant beauty.

A few moments later, I turned and faced the hotel, admiring its lines, loving the idea of being part of it. I'd missed Rhonda and couldn't wait for her to get back from her weekend away.

"Hello," came a voice alongside me.

I faced Catarina. "Hello. I'm happy to see you. It's a lovely time of day to be here."

"A quiet place to think." She let out a sigh. "You have a daughter too?"

"Yes, I do. My daughter, Liz, is around the same age as Philippa. She's married with four children and lives in town. I'm very blessed to have her so close to me."

"That's wonderful for you. I face a very different situation. I have no idea whether Philippa will remain here in Florida as she says or will decide to do something else. It's the first time, though, that she's found someone who she's very serious about. But then, how serious can you be in such a short period of time?"

"It's hard to face losing a daughter," I said sympathetically.

"She's resisted other offers," said Catarina. She shook her head and looked at the waves before turning back to me. "I guess I hate the idea of losing my daughter to a way of life I never envisioned for her."

"Philippa is a lovely young woman. You should be very proud of the job you've done with her. We're very excited about having her in our hotel family."

Catarina placed a hand on my shoulder. "Thank you for your kind words. I've never felt she should be bound by the promise between two old Italian men. That isn't fair. Enrico has tried to show respect for his elders, but this particular thing seems so silly."

"You can't plan someone else's happiness," I said. "It has to come from them. Just as you can't plan love."

"Oh, Ann, I hope we can become friends when I move to this area."

"The sale of the house has gone through?" I asked.

"Enrico is flying in today," Catarina said. "But I'm pretty sure he's going to agree that this is a perfect house for us. We'll keep an apartment in New York City, but I already think of Sabal as my new home."

"I'm so happy for you," I said, giving her a quick hug.

We walked along the beach together, each of us quiet as we settled into our own thoughts. I glanced at Catarina out of the corner of my eye and was glad she wanted to be friends.

"By the way, Luciano and Harper came on a sail with my husband and son yesterday. They are very cute together and are obviously attracted to one another."

"I'm happy for Luciano. He's a fine young man who's been wanting a chance away from family to make some decisions of his own," said Catarina. "He's not bound to the vineyard like his brothers."

"It's too early to tell what will happen to this relationship, but both Vaughn and I were impressed by their mutual behavior."

Catarina smiled but didn't say anything.

I checked my watch and said, "I must head back. I can't miss our executive meeting."

Catarina beamed at me. "I'm so happy I happened to see you."

"Me, too." I rushed back to the hotel. Bernie didn't like it if we were late to his meeting.

That afternoon, I checked the weekly calendar. Until an important dinner on Thursday, my schedule was lighter than usual, which made my idea of spending as much time as I could with Vaughn feasible. The only problem was the weather forecast.

A hurricane had formed off the African coast and might be heading to Florida. Though the track of the storm was unpredictable. I was concerned, but not overly worried. Fall months in Florida were often filled with uncertainty about the weather, and though we'd keep alert, we'd wait and see until the system moved closer.

As soon as I made sure everything was in order at the office, I left.

When I arrived home to surprise Vaughn, he wasn't there. But Cindy greeted me with her usual enthusiasm. I decided to work in the kitchen. It had been awhile since I'd done some cooking, and I knew Vaughn and Robbie loved my chicken casserole.

A short time later, Vaughn arrived home with Robbie.

"Ah, a pleasant surprise to see you here," said Vaughn kissing me.

"I'm making one of your favorite meals," I said. "For both of you. How did school go today?"

"Fine," said Robbie. "They're having another fall dance this weekend, and Brett and I decided we'd go."

"Sounds like fun. Do you have to invite a girl?" I asked, amused by the way Robbie's cheeks had turned pink.

"No," he said. "A group of us guys will go and hang out."

"Okay. Tell Brett's mother I'll be glad to share driving," I said as Robbie grabbed a snack from the cupboard and then left the room.

"Where does the time go?" Vaughn said. "Didn't we just bring him in the family? And now he's doing more and more on his own."

"It's fabulous for us to have so many grandchildren. They will keep us young," I said, realizing Robbie would be driving in what would seem no time at all.

Vaughn drew me to him. "You're the sexiest grandmother I know. Don't forget it."

I laughed as his lips met mine for a longer kiss than before, reminding me that as long as we thought of ourselves as young, the better we'd feel.

Later, just as Vaughn and I were heading to bed, I got a call from Rhonda. "Hi, Annie. We're back in town. Thought you'd want to know. Did I miss out on anything?"

"Nothing I can't tell you tomorrow. Did you have a delightful trip?"

"The best. Will, the old rooster, still has it," said Rhonda, and I couldn't help laughing.

We ended the call, and I laughed all over again telling Vaughn about it.

CHAPTER TWENTY-TWO

THE NEXT MORNING, I WAS IN THE KITCHEN LINGERING over a cup of coffee when I received a phone call from Bernie.

Surprised he was calling so early, I said, "Hi. What's up?"

"We've had some damage done to the sunset deck and building," said Bernie. "I think you and Rhonda need to look at this before we try to clean it up. We want to get it done right away so our guests won't see it."

"Have you called her?" I asked.

"No, I thought you might like to do that," said Bernie. "I know she just got back from vacation. This is a pretty upsetting way to return to work."

I hated to have Rhonda start her return to work this way but I knew Bernie was right. It was better to have this come from me. I punched her number on my cell.

"Hi, Rhonda. I've received some bad news about damage done to the sunset deck and building from Bernie. He wants us to meet him there right away."

"Now?" she asked.

"Yes, Sorry to start off the week for you this way. But he said they want to get it cleaned up before guests see it."

"Do you know what it is?"

"No, Bernie wanted us to take a look at it ourselves before they start the cleanup."

"Okay. I'm on my way," said Rhonda uncharacteristically quiet.

I said goodbye to Vaughn and Robbie and headed out. A niggling thought wormed its way through my body, but I told myself not to jump to any preconceived notions.

I made it to the hotel in record time and parked my car.

Just as I was ready to head down to the beach, Rhonda pulled into a space beside me. I waited for her to get out of the car, and we headed down the boardwalk together.

"I've got a bad feeling about this," said Rhonda.

"Me too," I admitted and stopped short.

THE BEACH HOUSE SUCKS!
COME EAT AT OSTERIA ARNO

was spray painted in black across the back of the wooden structure facing our guests as they walked to the beach.

Bernie saw us and waved us forward.

Across the front of the building was an arrow pointing up the beach and the words

OSTERIA ARNO IS THE BEST.

"What the fuck?" cried Rhonda. "Jonny Arno's people did this. Have you called the police?"

"And the insurance company?" I added.

"Yes, to both," said Bernie. "Security is trying to look through camera films, but both cameras were covered with black paint, so they're pretty useless."

Rhonda clutched her hands into fists. Her voice was icy. "They're not going to get away with this. We've put up with their shit long enough."

I put a hand on her shoulder. "Let's allow security and others do their job."

Tears shone in Rhonda's eyes, but she agreed.

"Take plenty of photos from all angles," I told Bernie, and then led Rhonda away. Beneath her sometimes tough stance was a tenderhearted person who was hurt by this.

We went to the hotel kitchen where Consuela was working. "I heard about the damage. Is it bad?"

"It can easily be fixed, but it's outrageous behavior," I said.

"That asshole is going to pay for this," Rhonda said, her eyes narrowing.

"I'm so sorry this happened. Have a warm roll and some coffee," said Consuela. "Maybe that will make you feel better."

"Thanks," I said, handing a cup of coffee to Rhonda and serving one for myself. It would take more than this to get rid of the way my stomach was twisting with nerves. This conflict with Jonny Arno needed to end.

We went into the office, where I gave Rhonda a rundown on the wedding and an update on the romance news from our two couples.

"Ah, I knew there was something going on with Luciano and Harper," said Rhonda. "I can sense these things, ya know?"

"Oh, yes. You remind me every time," I teased.

Rhonda chuckled and then grew serious. "I hereby predict everything will turn out fine for Philippa and Chet. But Philippa and Luciano have to convince their grandparents that an old family promise isn't meant to be kept. I know how much I worshipped my Italian grandparents. It won't be easy."

"How I envy those people who grew up with real families. You and your brother had a special experience," I said. "I guess that's why my hotel family is so important to me."

Rhonda gave me a steady look. "You know I can't let this business with Jonny Arno go. In a way, I must protect my family's reputation."

"Isn't that's carrying it a bit too far," I began and stopped when Rhonda glared at me.

"No, Annie. I'm not letting this go," she said. "In fact, a little later this morning I'm going to drive over to the restaurant and have a talk with Jonny about it."

Knowing it was useless to try and change her mind, I

sighed. "Then I'm going with you. I'd never let you put yourself in danger dealing with Jonny alone."

For the next few hours, we worked on numbers and plans for the week.

Rhonda rose. "Okay, Jonny should be at the restaurant by now. Let's go."

"Are you sure about this?" I asked, aware I couldn't stop her.

"You bet your ass," said Rhonda and led me outside.

Rhonda studied our automobiles. "Why don't you drive? Everyone in town knows my car." Rhonda's classic Cadillac convertible stood out.

We got into my car and headed to the restaurant, intent on settling our disagreement once and for all. Neither one of us wanted to continue to live this way.

When we pulled into the parking lot, we saw that it was empty except for Jonny's flashy gold-colored car and a large black SUV with tinted windows parked beside it.

"Good timing," said Rhonda. "Park here, away from the others so we can make a quick getaway."

I did as she said, and we got out of the car and headed toward the front doors.

Another large black SUV with tinted windows screeched up behind us, then pulled around in front of us, blocking our way.

A man jumped out of the back seat of the car and ran over to us.

"Get the fuck out of here," he snarled pointing to our car. He wore black clothing and sunglasses, reminding me of a few characters in detective movies.

"Hold on," said another man approaching us. He stopped and stared at us with surprise.

"What are you doing here, Vinnie Carozza?" said Rhonda wide-eyed.

"Rhonda DelMonte? We need to get both of them away from here ASAP," Vinnie said to the other man. "You go with them and take them to my hotel room. Now!"

I stared at the men and couldn't help noticing the shoulder gun holsters they wore.

"Who are you?" I asked trying to pull out of the grip of the man ordered to take us away.

"Get in your car, and drive where I tell you." The man clasped my arm even harder.

I glanced over at Rhonda. She was as scared as I was.

As soon as we climbed into the front seats of the car as he directed, the man sat in the back. "Hand me your phones."

It took us a minute to get them out of our purses, but we did as he asked.

"What's Vinnie got to do with this?" Rhonda asked him.

"I can't tell you. Now let's get out of here. We're going to travel south to Marco Island. I assume you know how to get there. When we do, I'll direct you from there. Don't try to draw attention to us," the man warned. "If you do, it could be dangerous for all of us. What were you doing at the restaurant, anyway?"

"We were going to talk to Jonny about the latest thing he's done to us," said Rhonda.

"Our property was defaced by his people," I said. "It really makes no sense at all. We're not out to fight with him."

"Sounds like him," said the man. "Let's hurry. I don't want you two involved in anything we're doing."

"Who's we?" asked Rhonda.

"I can't tell you that," the man answered. "Just keep your cool and no one will get hurt." He checked the rear view mirror. "I don't think anyone saw us or is following."

My fingers gripped the steering wheel so hard they hurt. It was difficult to resist doing something unexpected to get rid of the man. But I thought of Vaughn and my children and knew I'd never try. We'd been warned of the danger, and I definitely had the impression the person had a gun and would have no problem using it.

I glanced at Rhonda and shook my head, indicating how I felt.

She'd folded her fingers into fists and knew she was mad as hell.

Doing as he'd ordered; I drove south and onto the island. Then to a small hotel at the water's edge he directed us to.

"Okay, we're clear. Park and get out," he ordered. "We'll walk directly across the parking lot to the entrance of the ground-floor room we want. Remember, no problems."

Feeling queasy. I got out of the car and stood on unsteady feet until Rhonda joined me. Then we walked together, the man right behind us.

A woman in the distance waved to us from a nearby dock and I automatically waved back.

"Move it," said the man quietly. "Go to the door right in front of us."

He gave us warning looks as he indicated we were to step aside and then he quickly unlocked the door and waved us inside.

"Okay, you can relax now," the man said. "You're safe as long as you don't do anything to draw attention to us. No phone calls, no stepping outside to the deck. Vinnie will be here shortly." He pulled his gun out of his shoulder holster.

"May I use the restroom?" I asked politely.

"Okay, but again, no trying to call attention to us. It's important to you and your family. Understand?"

I glanced at Rhonda. Neither one of us would do anything

to harm them.

We both freshened up and then sat on a couch watching television. When Rhonda found an old run of *The Sins of the Children*, the soap opera Vaughn had starred in for years, my eyes filled with tears. I'd been too frightened to cry, but now that we were considered safe by the man who'd kidnapped us, I couldn't help it.

If Rhonda and I got out of this situation alive, I knew how relieved Vaughn would be. But when he learned the details of our ordeal, he'd be upset that Rhonda and I had once again got caught up in another troublesome mess.

CHAPTER TWENTY-THREE

AFTER WHAT SEEMED A LIFETIME BUT WAS IN TRUTH under an hour, two men dressed in black entered the hotel room with Vinnie, a tall man with brown hair. When he took off his jacket, I noticed his broad shoulders and well-exercised body.

"Everything all right, here?" Vinnie asked our guard. Concern showed in his brown eyes.

"They're safe, and we haven't drawn attention," said the man.

Rhonda stood with her hands on her hips. "Vinnie Carozza, tell me what's going on. What kind of trouble are we in?"

"We've saved you from a lot of it. Don't worry, I wouldn't let anything bad happen to you. You and your brother always stood up for me in the neighborhood. Your mom's cooking helped me too." Smiling, he walked over to her and gave her a hug. "It's nice to see you. I've read all about you and your partner owning and running the hotel. Someday I might even have the chance to stay there."

Rhonda gazed at him. "Have you gone over to the dark side?"

He shook his head. "No, my men and I are here for the government. We heard about a meeting between Jonny and a man we've been looking for. I'm afraid it didn't go well for either of them. Jonny was shot dead, and the other man was wounded and taken into our custody."

I suddenly realized what a favor he'd done for us by getting us away from the restaurant. "Thank you, Vinnie. That could've been awful for us to witness."

"And a chance for you to ruin things and maybe get killed," he answered. "I'm very glad we intercepted you in time to get you away from the scene. You can have your phones back to call whoever you need to. But you can't leave until we get statements from you regarding your ongoing difficulties with Jonny."

We were given our phones, and I immediately called Vaughn.

"No details," said Vinnie, warning us both.

When Vaughn answered, I couldn't help the tears that spilled down my cheeks. I'd been more frightened than I'd thought. Simply hearing his voice reminded me of how much I loved him, how safe he made me feel.

"Hi, Ann. What's wrong?" he asked.

"I'm just calling to tell you that I'm away from the office. Rhonda and I are together being interviewed about damage that was done to the hotel. I'll call you again before we leave the meeting to come home, but it may be a while."

"You sound stressed. Are you sure you're alright?" he said.

I drew a deep breath and calmed myself. "I'm fine. I'll tell you all about it later."

I ended the call and sat as Rhonda continued speaking to Will.

I decided to phone Bernie so he wouldn't spread news about Rhonda and me missing scheduled meetings. I had to leave a message for him. I told him Rhonda and I were away from the hotel but would return as soon as we could.

Vinnie shot me a look of his approval. "Okay, ladies, what can we get you for lunch? We'll do our best to get you through all this, but we have to be sure we have as many details prior to the 'take down' as possible."

One of the men who'd changed into less conspicuous

clothing was now wearing shorts and a golf shirt. "I'll get whatever you want."

"I'd like iced tea and a Caesar salad with shrimp," I said realizing that after the stress had eased, I was hungry.

"I'll have the same," said Rhonda. "But I'm tellin' ya that after the day we've had, I'm going to have a cocktail tonight."

We all laughed, relieved the situation with Jonny had been taken out of our hands.

Later, Rhonda and I were grilled as we ate our lunches on the couch, answering questions about any interactions we'd had with Jonny.

"Who else was on his team?" Vinnie asked leaning forward in a chair in front of us.

Rhonda and I studied each other, then Rhonda said, "Brock Goodwin."

"Yes, he was quoted in the local newspaper as saying something to the effect that The Beach House Hotel wouldn't be able to compete with Osteria Arno. We'll be talking to him a bit later."

I pressed my lips together, loving the idea.

Rhonda winked at me, and I saw that she was having the same reaction as me. After all he'd done, Brock deserved any harassment Vinnie intended to give him.

"Guess he's a pain in the ass to the two of you, huh?" Vinnie said.

"You could say that," Rhonda said. "Have you been planning this raid on Jonny for a while?"

"More on the man he met with," said Vinnie. "But no one liked what Jonny was doing. He was squandering money, causing problems where none should exist, and drawing unwanted attention. The people he'd promised to produce for were fed up."

"What will happen to the restaurant?" I asked.

Vinnie shrugged. "They'll probably sell it. One of the private investors is interested. Maybe change the name and bring in a new chef."

My mind spun. *A new, young chef?*

We answered a few more questions, then Vinnie stood. "Thank you for your help. You can go now. But I warn you that nothing can be said about this. If anything gets out about our conversations and the raid itself, our investigation could be ruined. We wouldn't take kindly to such a thing happening."

"What about our husbands? I know they're worried about us," I said.

"Does the local media know?" asked Rhonda.

"They know that Jonny has been killed. That's all. We've said it was a shooting. Say as little as possible and don't give away anything that can be used against us. We won't divulge your names to any lawyers other than our own and only if necessary."

Rhonda and Vinnie hugged. "It was great to see you," she said. "If you want some decent Italian food with recipes from my mother and my nonna, you know where to reach me. I'd love for you to meet my husband and children."

"Sounds like something a single man like me would really appreciate," he said. "Thanks. I'll let you know. I see your brother from time to time at the butcher shop."

"He's doing well," said Rhonda.

I faced him. "Thanks for your help in keeping Rhonda and me safe."

He tipped his head. "Always ready to do that."

He walked us to the door and showed us out. "Safe travels."

Rhonda and I trotted to my car, opened it, and climbed in.

"Wow! What a shitty day," said Rhonda, clasping her hands

to her cheeks. "I thought we were goners until I saw Vinnie. Then I calmed down a little."

I held out my hands in front of me and saw they were still shaking. "I didn't calm down one bit. They had guns. I kept wondering what we'd gotten ourselves into."

"I think it's more about what we got ourselves out of," said Rhonda. "I knew Jonny Arno was trouble from the beginning. I'm sorry he was killed, but I'm not that surprised. He was a foolish man to think he could disrespect his backers that way. He let his ego get in the way of making decent choices."

"Amen," I said. "Now, let's go home."

CHAPTER TWENTY-FOUR

I DIDN'T KNOW HOW JONNY'S DEATH WOULD BE described in various news reports, but I hoped it was made clear that The Beach House Hotel had nothing to do with it. Rhonda and I had worked too hard to be embroiled in a murder.

"We have to meet with Bernie. News like this is important, and we'll want him to be able to make some kind of statement, speaking for us," I said.

"You're right. After all the news of the conflict between us, the media will want some reaction from the hotel."

We pulled into my parking spot at the rear of the hotel and went inside directly to Bernie's office.

We knocked on his door and opened it.

Bernie looked up and waved for us to come inside while continuing to talk on the phone. "Terri, I'll have to get back to you. Yes, we understand the fairness of letting you know our reaction to such news."

With a bewildered look, Bernie said, "Did you know Jonny Arno was killed today?"

"That's what we want to talk to you about," said Rhonda.

"We heard about it and want to prepare a media statement about the Beach House Hotel's reaction to it."

"We can't say we're pleased?" teased Bernie, which coming from him was a huge joke. "By the way, the graffiti was covered up on the sunset building early this morning."

"That may make things easier," I said. "We want to be sympathetic to the killing without saying much about the so-called competition between us."

"Wise decision. Polite, a bit aloof. Got it," said Bernie. "Why don't I handle it and give a draft to you to look over before I make a statement? We'll also increase security here at the hotel."

"Thank you, Bernie," I said. "Rhonda and I are going home."

"We'll see you tomorrow," Rhonda said. "Thanks for your help."

We rose and left the office.

"I feel as if I've lived a lifetime since this morning," I said to Rhonda throwing an arm around her shoulder. "It's a good thing we ran into your childhood friend."

"It's just like Nonna told me many times," said Rhonda. "How you treat people can become a blessing or a curse. This time it was a big blessing."

We went to our cars and headed to our homes.

As I pulled into my driveway, Vaughn emerged from the house with Cindy at his heels.

I parked the car and got out. Without saying anything, I went into his arms.

Vaughn hugged me and then studied my face. "I heard on the news that Jonny Arno was killed. Did that have anything to do with you?

"No," I said. "But we had graffiti damage done to the sunset building this morning. I think it was done by an amateur, perhaps one of Jonny's supporters."

"I'm sorry he was killed, but Jonny Arno was a despicable man," said Vaughn.

"I'd heard the rumor that his backers weren't happy with him," I said. "I'm not sure we'll ever know all the real facts, but I understand he was fired for ruining business at Chez Michel's, the restaurant in Miami. I also heard he bought a flashy new car and overspent on Osteria Arno. I'm guessing that was just the beginning of his troubles."

"I wouldn't be surprised. Something was off with that whole restaurant deal. I want you to promise me you'll be especially watchful about the people around you."

"Bernie has promised to increase security at the hotel, and I feel perfectly safe here at home with you," I said.

"I was able to delay my business trip again but then I have to leave," said Vaughn.

"No problem." I didn't want him to know anything about the day's activities.

"Come on inside," said Vaughn. "Let's go for a swim in the pool and relax.

He had no idea how wonderful that sounded to me.

Later that night, after Robbie had gone to bed, I sat in Vaughn's lap on the lanai cuddling with him. Life could be full of cruelty and unhappiness but being with him made me happy and mentally prepared to move forward.

After I awoke from a restless night of nightmares, I tiptoed away from the bed and prepared for a walk on the beach. It would be another step in getting rid of the ugliness of yesterday's events.

While Vaughn and Robbie slept, I quietly left the house and drove to the hotel. After all the tension caused by Jonny's behavior, I was ready to begin the day with a fresh outlook, one without worry.

When I pulled into my parking space behind the hotel, I was surprised to see Rhonda's car there. Curious, I went inside to talk to her.

She was sitting in the office at her computer.

"Hi, what are you doing here so early?" I asked.

Rhonda shook her head and sighed. "I couldn't sleep. I kept thinking how close we'd been to a disaster if we'd entered the restaurant. We might've been killed by either man."

I plopped down in my desk chair and faced her. "My dreams last night were exactly about that. I couldn't wait to leave the house and get here. A walk on the beach might help us both."

Rhonda got to her feet. "I was hoping you'd be here early. Let's do it."

We left the building and walked out onto the sand. The sun was a glowing orb in the sky, a symbol of promise. As usual, joggers and shell collectors were present, but it was an excellent time and place for us to unwind. The hotel business was full of surprises and interesting people. Not all of them were satisfying experiences.

As we stood looking out at the water, Rhonda spoke. "Ya know, Annie, I've been thinking. We've gone through a lot of ups and downs, but I wouldn't want to be in business with anyone but you. More than that, you're my best friend."

"And you are mine," I said turning and giving her a hug.

"Well, well, what is this? A love fest for two?" came a familiar voice we hated.

Brock jogged up to us.

"Did you hear about Jonny Arno? It's all over the news," said Rhonda, and I knew she was trying to find out how Jonny's death might affect him.

Brock drew a deep breath and kicked at the sand with the toe of his sneaker in an uncharacteristic vulnerable pose. "Yes, it's a real shame. I'm still trying to come to terms with it. No matter what Jonny told others, we were business partners."

"Of a kind," I said. I knew that instead of putting money

into the enterprise, he'd donated items from his import business.

He grimaced. "Yeah. I don't know what's going to happen with the restaurant." He studied Rhonda. "You women certainly didn't help. I heard you were offering a special Italian dinner at the hotel. Wasn't that going a little overboard on competition with Jonny?"

"All the restaurants in the area do what's right for them. That's how they survive in a competitive market," I said quickly.

"Yeah, mind your own damn business," said Rhonda unable to hold back.

"Don't think your troubles are going away. I have a job to do as president of the Neighborhood Association," said Brock getting back his fighting spirit.

"You be careful yourself," said Rhonda.

He gazed at the sunset building and said, "Good that you got that graffiti covered up, huh?"

My eyes widened, and I sent Rhonda a silent message not to say anything.

"*Ciao*," said Brock waving to us before taking off in a jog down the beach.

Watching him go, Rhonda muttered, "That ass!"

I grabbed hold of her arm. "Listen. Brock talked about cleaning up the graffiti. How did he know it was there? We saw it early in the morning. Earlier than this time. And Bernie said they got it cleaned up right away."

"You think he had something to do with it?" Rhonda asked.

"Maybe he didn't do it, but I think he knew about it," I said.

"It wouldn't surprise me," said Rhonda. "C'mon, I've got to walk off some of my anger."

###

We headed up the beach, past the guesthouses, to the next major hotel and then turned around and walked back to our own.

As we returned, Catarina called to us and walked our way.

"Ann and Rhonda, I'm so glad I saw you. Enrico has returned to The Beach House Hotel with two very important guests. Philippa's and Luciano's grandfathers. They're staying in the guesthouse with Enrico and me, and I want to do something special for them. Like the dinner you had for Enrico."

I turned to Rhonda.

A sparkle returned to her eyes, and I could see her mind working.

Sure enough, she said, "I have an even better idea. I'd like to invite all of you in the family to my house for dinner tomorrow evening. Chet and I will prepare a similar meal there."

"Oh, that would be fantastic," said Catarina. "I want both men to see what a delightful place this hotel is and why we'd want to buy a house here. Tomorrow is perfect. They'll have had a chance to rest a little after their flights."

"Are they here about the kids?" Rhonda asked.

"They're here, in part, to see for themselves that their intended plan would never work. Seeing the kids and talking face-to-face will help settle this situation. It was a sweet dream between two dear old friends and the wives they loved. That's all."

"We're delighted they're here," I said. "Hopefully, they'll spread the word about our hotel. We love having international visitors."

Catarina chuckled. "They both have large extended families. It could be a very lucrative thing for you."

"I will give you a call later to officially welcome you to

dinner at my house," said Rhonda. "I need to get permission from Jean-Luc and others to have Chet and Philippa available. We'll check on Harper and Luciano."

"Thank you. A visit to your home is a lovely gesture," said Catarina, turning as two white-haired men made their way to the sand. "Here the grandfathers are now. Come meet Enrico's father, Angelo Ferrara, and our family friend, Giovanni Bolino."

We followed Catarina to greet them.

She made the introductions, and I couldn't help thinking how adorable the men were. Small in stature, their eyes held a hint of amusement as I shook hands with each of them.

"*Sei bellisssima,*" Giovanni said softly, smiling at me.

Angelo turned to him and nodded.

"You will be my guests," said Rhonda. "For true Italian food."

"Ah, *grazie mille,*" said Angelo.

"We'll see you tomorrow," said Catarina.

"Enjoy your day," I said, and followed Rhonda back to where we'd left our shoes.

Smiling gleefully, Rhonda rubbed her hands together. "This is going to be so fun. I'm so happy we're going to be a part of it."

"Hold on, we can't get too involved," I said.

"We'll see," said Rhonda, beginning to hum a song.

CHAPTER TWENTY-FIVE

WE ENTERED THE HOTEL AND WENT DIRECTLY TO THE kitchen. Jean-Luc had returned to duty wearing a special leg brace. He was determined not to lose control of his domain, and we didn't blame him.

We told him about the dinner Rhonda and Chet would work on at Rhonda's house and he had no problem with Chet working there. He was in training, after all.

"It's wonderful to see you back," I said. "But don't overdo it or Lindsay will be upset with not only you but with Rhonda and me."

He laughed. "Believe me, she was glad to have me out of the house. And she knows how much I love my work here at the hotel."

"You rest when you need to," said Rhonda. "Use the chairs in the breakroom."

We installed a couple of lounge chairs there. For people working on their feet all day, it was a way to give their backs and legs some relief.

We went to Consuela's part of the kitchen to get coffee and a treat.

"Hello, ladies," she said. "You're getting an early start to the day. What do you think about the news of Jonny being killed?"

"I think he made too many enemies," said Rhonda.

"Still, I was surprised," I said.

Consuela shook her head. "He was not well-liked. His staff hated working there. I don't know what will happen with that restaurant. It's bound to be better."

Rhonda and I accepted the plates she handed us and grabbed our cups of coffee.

We were sitting in the office when Rhonda's cell phone rang.

She frowned at it and picked up the call. "Rhonda Grayson."

A smile broke across her face. "Hi, Vinnie. Thanks for calling. Yes, Ann and I are fine, but I want to thank you again for taking us away from what could've been a nasty situation."

She listened and turned to me. "Vinnie wants to know if we remember anything else he should know about."

I let out a long sigh. "I think you should tell him about our encounter with Brock. I think he may know something about the graffiti."

"I agree," Rhonda said and told Vinnie our suspicions. "Really?" she said. "Okay, if we think of anything else, we'll call you at this number. Thanks again. I meant it when I said come visit us."

Rhonda ended the call and turned to me. "Vinnie said they're looking into tax problems with Brock."

I lifted my shoulders and let them drop. "He never learns."

"Brock may be off our backs for a while. Sounds like he's in more trouble than we thought," said Rhonda. "After we finish our coffee, let's walk over to Chet's apartment and talk to him about tomorrow. We'll want our two couples there."

As Rhonda and I stood outside the apartment, we could hear voices inside. We knocked and Harper came to the door. "Hello. Come on in. The four of us are discussing the latest news."

"My mother called to tell me that my grandfather and

Luciano's are here visiting," said Philippa. "She told me about Rhonda's plan to have us all come for dinner tomorrow night."

"And for me to help you create an Italian dinner at your home," said Chet.

"Yes," said Rhonda. "It will be more informal, more comfortable at my house. I have a professional kitchen with enough space so we can work together on the meal."

"It's important for all of you to be there," I said. "You'll need to request time off from your jobs. Luciano, I understand you're going to be working in the dining room as a wine steward."

He nodded and smiled. "I did a trial service last night."

"Okay," said Rhonda. "Chet will be working with me tomorrow and all of you will come to dinner. I'll ask you to arrive a few minutes early for a six o'clock dinner."

"Make it an excellent dinner. We want our grandfathers to be in a jovial mood," said Philippa.

"Absolutely," I said, and then Rhonda and I left.

Rhonda and I reported the latest to Bernie and returned to our office to work on finances and marketing for Thanksgiving and Christmas. Thankfully, the private dinner that had been scheduled was moved to the following week, and I wouldn't have to worry about that.

As a way to include them, Rhonda asked Liz to come up with individually designed and printed menu cards for tomorrow's dinner guests. Angela agreed to make the dessert—Rhonda's special tiramisu.

Vaughn had already delayed his trip, so he could attend the dinner. It was important to Rhonda and me to have him there. We hadn't discussed it, but this dinner affected all of us and the pleasant outcome we hoped to achieve. We'd just have to wait to see how it worked out.

The next morning while I worked in the office I was surprised by a visit from Enrico.

"I hope I'm not interrupting anything," he said.

"Not at all. I'm just doing my usual work," I said. "Won't you sit down? Can I help you with something?"

He took a seat in a chair in front of my desk. "I'm here because I want you and Rhonda to know that I'm one of the people who invested in Osteria Arno as a favor to a friend. I and others are very sorry for the way Jonny tried to engage in unhealthy competition. With his death, I'm not sure what will happen to the restaurant, but I wanted you to be aware of my connection to it."

"Thank you for telling me. Rhonda and I have no hard feelings at all toward the restaurant and the people behind it. We simply never wanted to be lured into Jonny's idea of competition. We are pleased to have Jean-Luc at the hotel."

"And now you have Chet Waring," said Enrico.

"For the moment," I said. "He's been training with Jean-Luc, and we like him a lot. How do you like the house Catarina has chosen?"

Enrico smiled his approval. "I think it's perfect for us. I might never have thought of moving to Sabal if I hadn't been approached to invest in a restaurant here. But having visited and done some research, I became happy with the idea."

"It's nice that your father and his friend can visit. Catarina was pleased they could see for themselves that it's a wise decision."

"Yes, I'm glad, too," said Enrico. "The two men are old and want their families to be settled."

"In this day with everyone traveling and exploring new

opportunities, I'm not sure that's possible. It's certainly risky to try and predict the best outcome."

"True, true," said Enrico getting to his feet. "Thanks for your time. I'll see you tonight at dinner."

"I can't wait. Chet and Rhonda's Italian cooking is the best," I said.

"Their dinner at the hotel was fantastic." He gave a polite bob of his head goodbye and left the office.

Sitting alone again, I thought it might be wise to talk to Rhonda about this news tomorrow. Today, she'd need all her energy to prepare for the elegant meal she planned at her home.

Liz called to say that she and Chad had been invited to the dinner.

"It will be a special evening out. There will be sixteen of us," Liz said. "I'm working on the menu cards now."

"I'm looking forward to it myself," I said. "How are the kids?"

"Fine," Liz said. "The Ts are loving kindergarten and I'm happy to have some alone time with Gabe. It's so easy with him."

I laughed. "Don't you sometimes wonder how you did it with the triplets? It makes being with one so easy."

"Maybe it's the baby thing, too. He's my last one."

"I know how that feels. For me, you were my last and only one." I sighed at the memory of those times I couldn't carry those other children to term. The pain was real.

"I've got to go," said Liz. "One more thing. Any chance I could borrow one of your sundresses?"

"Sure. Why don't you and Gabe meet me at my house for lunch, and we'll pick one together? I'll bring salads from the hotel and fix Gabe something."

"Thanks, Mom. See you in a bit."

We ended the call, and I thought, as I often did, how lucky I was to have Liz and her family living in Sabal.

CHAPTER TWENTY-SIX

THAT EVENING, VAUGHN AND I ARRIVED AT RHONDA'S house early so we'd be able to greet her guests together.

Stepping out of Vaughn's car I inhaled the tantalizing aromas coming from the kitchen. "M-m-m, delicious."

Vaughn took my arm. "I've waited all day for this dinner. Rhonda never disappoints."

"Chet's helping too. I'm hoping that will enhance the grandfathers' opinions of him."

"All this matchmaking. Do you think it'll help?" teased Vaughn.

I gave him a thumbs up. "I hope so. The kids want it to happen."

Rhonda's daughter, Willow, greeted us at the door dressed in a pretty pink dress. Her features and body type were a mixture of both parents. Her temperament, too. I was her godmother and adored her.

"Hi, Auntie Ann and Uncle Vaughn. Welcome," she said in a very ladylike pose before throwing herself into my arms.

I hugged her. "You did such a nice job of greeting us."

"Thanks. Drew and I promised Mom we'd behave," she said.

"Where's Drew?" I asked. At ten, Drew was two years younger than Willow and was a much quieter kid.

"He's helping Philippa with the table," Willow answered with self-importance. "Won't you come in?"

As we walked past, Vaughn stopped to give Willow a loving pat on the back.

Rhonda's large house was gorgeous. Seating sixteen people for dinner was a challenge she could meet.

Looking into the dining room, I saw that the large table was covered by a white linen cloth with soft green napkins to match the gold and green trim on the china. Crystal water goblets and wine glasses sat at each place. On top of each serving plate was a printed menu with a guest's name.

In the middle of the table sat a low arrangement of hibiscus flowers and greenery.

Rhonda walked over to me.

I gave her a hug. "Everything looks fabulous as usual."

"And smells delicious," said Vaughn, quickly kissing her.

Will walked into the room, kissed me on the cheek, and shook hands with Vaughn. The two men, so different in personalities, liked one another, which made for congenial times when we got together.

"Come say hi to Chet and Philippa," said Rhonda. "They've been working in the kitchen all day. Philippa wanted to make her grandmother's wedding soup for a starter."

"Hi, Auntie Ann and Uncle Vaughn," said Drew walking into the room.

I hugged him and then stood back. "My, Drew. I think you're going to be tall like your father."

A shy smile crossed his face. "Taller than Willow."

I chuckled. Drew might be quieter, but he wasn't going to let Willow beat him at anything.

Vaughn gave him a clap on the back. "Ready to go on another sail with Robbie and me?"

"Sure," said Drew.

We followed Rhonda into her large, professional kitchen. Wearing identical green aprons, Chet and Philippa greeted me.

"It smells delicious," I said. "I have a feeling the

grandfathers will be impressed."

"Luciano and Harper have selected the wines," said Rhonda. "They should be arriving any moment. The red Barolo wine has already been decanted."

I turned as Luciano and Harper entered the kitchen. "Great to see you again," I said as Luciano kissed me French style on one cheek and then the other.

As Harper and I hugged, she whispered, "I'm so nervous."

"Don't be," I said quietly, firmly. "You'll be fine."

She nodded and then greeted Vaughn.

I realized that for the four of these young people, putting on a delicious dinner was much more than that. I wanted to tell them to just relax and be themselves. But there was no time to do so, as Willow ran into the kitchen to announce that cars were arriving.

Rhonda signaled me, and we walked to the front of the house to welcome them as we did our guests at the hotel.

Vaughn and Will joined us, and we stepped outside where we'd have more room to greet and introduce the new arrivals.

Enrico and Catarina approached us, each holding onto the arm of one of the older gentlemen. I was touched by the elders' obvious effort to dress for the evening. They wore ties and jackets, and their silver hair was combed and brushed.

Liz and Chad, followed by Angie and Reggie, stepped forward.

More introductions were made.

"So nice to have the young people here," said Enrico's father, Angelo.

"Too many are leaving their homelands," added Giovanni, Luciano's grandfather.

"We're lucky," said Rhonda. "I thought I'd lose Angela and Reggie to New York, but they decided to stay here in Sabal."

Giovanni tightened his lips but said nothing. Still, his eyes brightened when he saw Luciano walking toward him, holding onto Harper's hand. "*Buonasera*," he said to them.

"Good evening, *Nonno*," said Luc. "You remember Harper from last night?"

Giovanni smiled at Harper. "A beautiful lady I never forget."

Rhonda and I gazed hopefully at one another. Was there acceptance there?

Angelo's face lit with pleasure as Philippa walked over and hugged him.

I noticed he hesitated a moment, then shook hands with Chet.

"Please come inside," said Will.

After everyone was seated at the table and served water and wine by two members of the dining staff whom we had hired for the evening, Will stood and raised his wine glass.

"Here's to a wonderful evening. We welcome Angelo and Giovanni and their families to Sabal. May it be the beginning of a long friendship."

"A new family," said Rhonda, her eyes sparkling with mischief.

I raised my glass to a toast and then took a sip of the wine. The evening was off to a congenial start.

Next, two platters of antipasti were served full of tasty tidbits to nibble on. I studied the selection of vegetables, meats, and cheeses and knew enough to take just a little. I'd need the room for Rhonda's veal and mushroom dish.

As the soup was being served, Philippa announced that it was her grandmother's recipe.

I watched as Angelo took his first sip of it. Beaming at Philippa he said, "Your *nonna* would be so proud. *Delizioso*."

His eyes watered, and when he caught me watching him, he returned my smile and shrugged, winning my affection.

Conversation was interesting as old family stories were told. I listened eagerly. I had little to contribute because of my situation. Rhonda winked at me knowing I felt a little out of my element.

"When Philippa was born, I knew she'd be right for my Luciano," said Giovanni. "That's why Angelo and I made this pact. It's what your grandmothers wanted too. Looking at you now, seeing how you've grown, I wish it was still possible."

"But *Nonno*, it can't be. Not for either of us," said Luciano. "You see how Philippa is with Chet. And Harper is my new girlfriend."

Enrico interceded. "We can discuss this later. Now is the time to enjoy this dinner."

Both older men nodded their agreement, and the conversation turned to Sabal and all its offerings.

When it came time for dessert, Angela explained that she'd learned to make tiramisu from her mother who'd learned it from her grandmother.

We ate it with pleasure and then Enrico stood holding his wine glass aloft. "We have truly found a reason to say we're family. All of us. Sharing a heavenly meal like this is like sharing souls. Thank you to all who've contributed to such a special one."

"Chet and I, Philippa, Luciano, and Harper have all made the dinner, but the rest of you have made the meal," said Rhonda.

As we lifted our glasses, I returned Vaughn's smile, aware he knew how much I loved it when I could extend my hotel family.

CHAPTER TWENTY-SEVEN

THE NEXT MORNING, I DROVE VAUGHN TO THE AIRPORT. He could easily have taken an Uber or limo, but it had become a routine for us because it gave us a special time alone. After the scare I'd had, I was more than happy to do it. His trip wouldn't be for long, but I always hated to see him go. The house was so empty without him.

As he kissed me at the drop-off spot, he murmured, "Stay out of trouble. Promise?"

I laughed. "I'll do my best. Don't worry. Everything is under control with Osteria Arno. Enrico stopped in the office yesterday to tell me he's a silent partner in the restaurant. He wanted to say how sorry he was for all that had happened to Rhonda and me regarding incidents at our hotel."

"Interesting. I like him and appreciate that honesty," said Vaughn. He kissed me again, retrieved his luggage from the backseat, and waved goodbye.

I drove directly to the hotel anxious to thank Rhonda for a fantastic dinner and to tell her about Enrico.

When I walked into our office, Rhonda held a finger to her lips as she listened to someone talk on the phone.

"I see. Ann just walked into the office. Hang on, and I'll tell you what we decide."

She turned to me with a grin. "Vinnie is on the phone. The FBI has been interviewing Brock about his participation in the defacing of our property, and he's wondering if we want to bring charges. Brock is the person who recruited someone to spray paint our building."

"You know what I'd like?" I told her, and chuckling softly, Rhonda went back on the call.

"You're on speaker phone now, Vinnie." Rhonda glanced at me. "Ann and I don't want to press charges. However, we'd like Brock to make a formal apology to us in your presence. Can you do that?"

"You bet. I've never met such an egotistical jackass. That's a better punishment for sure. I'll bring him around sometime this afternoon."

"Call us first, so we're ready," said Rhonda. "And, Vinnie, from one neighborhood kid to another, thank you."

She ended the call, and we gave each other a high five. How many times would it take for Brock to understand he couldn't bully us or try to hurt our business without our fighting back?

We'd just finished lunch when Vinnie called to tell us that he and Brock were on their way to the hotel.

"I can't wait to see and hear him grovel," said Rhonda, rubbing her hands together enthusiastically.

"We can't appear too smug," I warned her. "It might backfire on us."

"Aw, Annie, you take the fun out of it," Rhonda complained.

"Brock is capable of anything." I shuddered at the memory of how he'd accosted me on my one and only date with him when I was new to the area.

Rhonda sensed my worry. "Okay. I'll be good."

A knock sounded on our door and then Vinnie led Brock inside.

"'Afternoon," said Vinnie. "Thank you for being so kind as to not file charges against Brock Goodwin. I'm sure he'd like to say a few words."

Brock's cheeks turned bright red. He shuffled his feet and looked down at the floor.

When he raised his head, I saw defiance, not defeat, and I felt my hands grow cold even as heat burned in my belly.

"I think it might be better if we filed charges after all," I said, surprising Rhonda.

She looked from me to him. "I like that better too. It's much easier than listening to this liar."

Brock's eyes widened. He took a step backward and turned to Vinnie. "They're just saying that because I'm the president of the Neighborhood Association. They never want to listen to me."

"Can't say I blame them," said Vinnie. "You arranged to have graffiti painted on their property."

"Well, I ... I had an investment to protect," said Brock.

I shook my head. "We know how you made that investment by trading imported goods from your business for a percentage of the restaurant."

Vinnie's eyebrows lifted. "We haven't discussed that, Brock. But I'm sure the tax people will want to."

Brock's shoulders slumped. "All right, all right. I'm sorry I did that. Satisfied?"

"I'm not," said Vinnie. "You have to do a lot better than that."

"Okay," groaned Brock. "I won't do anything like that again. I promise."

"Do you promise to be a good neighbor?" asked Rhonda, enjoying his discomfort.

Vinnie nudged Brock.

"I promise," Brock said.

"Vinnie can be our witness," I said. "Time for you to stop interfering with our business."

"Thanks, Vinnie," said Rhonda as they turned to leave.

Brock whipped around. "You know this guy?"

Rhonda gave him a smug look. "I know lots of people. Goodbye, Brock."

We waited until they'd left before allowing ourselves to release our laughter.

For the next few days while Vaughn was gone, I devoted time to Robbie and to babysitting Liz's children whenever I could fit it into my schedule. Olivia, Emma, and Noah were so more grown-up than a few months ago when they'd left pre-school and entered kindergarten.

Being with them filled me with joy. Having had only Liz, it was fascinating to see how they interacted and talked to one another. Gabe tried to be part of the trio but was still too young to compete. But not too young for cuddles from me.

One afternoon, I sat on the patio with Liz watching the children play in the backyard.

"Did you ever think you'd end up with four children after trying so hard for one?" I asked her. "It seems like such a miracle."

"Definitely," she said. "But as tired as I get, I realize they're growing fast." She looked at them and grinned. "Can you imagine them as teenagers?"

I laughed. "That will be a challenge."

"Still, it will allow me to be part of the hotel operation," said Liz.

"Are you and Angela really going to be able to take over for Rhonda and me one day?"

"Yes," Liz said with no hesitation. "Right now, it's difficult to give the time to it. But I figure in a year or so, we'll be able to maintain a real schedule there. Now, with Harper gone for a few days, we've had to put our new plan on hold."

"Harper is away? Where did she go?" I asked.

Liz clapped a hand to her mouth. "Maybe I wasn't supposed to say anything, but she and Luciano flew to Ohio so he could meet her parents."

"Oh, my! Does Rhonda know? She'll say it was all her doing."

Laughing, Liz said, "No. I don't think she knows. Angela's better at keeping secrets than I am. You can't say anything to her, Mom."

"I won't, but you know Rhonda and I normally share any news we can," I said. "Do you think this trip is part of an engagement? They've only just met."

"I think it's more an old-fashioned thing, like asking if he can court her. They're both shy talking about it," Liz said. "But all you have to do is look at them together to see there's something real there."

"What about Philippa and Chet?" I asked. "Any news there?"

Liz shook her head. "Harper didn't say anything to me about them."

"Time will take care of things," I said. "It's been a very interesting fall so far."

"When is Vaughn coming back? Will you be able to take some time off?" Liz asked.

"He'll be back tomorrow," I said. "We'll relax at home, and then we'll see."

Liz took hold of my hand. "It's wonderful to see you two happy together. I remember how it was with Dad."

"Me too. I'm lucky to have found Vaughn," I said. "And if you hadn't roomed with Angela at college, where would we be?"

"Probably not in Sabal, Florida," she said smiling and waving to her children.

CHAPTER TWENTY-EIGHT

THE NEXT MORNING, AFTER DROPPING ROBBIE OFF AT school, I headed to the beach. I needed that private time to sort out my thoughts.

As I usually did, I parked my car, took off my shoes, and headed to the beach. Feeling the crystals of sand between my toes, my body loosened. Vaughn would be home this afternoon and I could truly relax, knowing he'd be my support and help me see things more clearly.

I walked down to the water and lifted my face to the sun. Shards of yellow from the sun coated the tips of the waves as they rolled in to shore. It was magical. And when the birds above me cried out it added a musical touch to the moment

Letting out a long sigh I felt my lips curve. Being here was such a treasure.

I turned away from the water and began my walk.

The sound of my feet hitting the hard-packed sand at the water's edge made a rhythmic beat below me.

In the distance I could see Brock Goodwin and debated turning around. But I couldn't let him see how uncomfortable he made me.

As we got closer, he noticed me and walked away. I stopped in surprise. This was a first. Maybe being forced to be neighborly was a bigger punishment for him than Rhonda and I had believed possible.

Deep in thought, I headed back to the hotel.

Catarina emerged from the guesthouse where she and her family were staying.

I waved, and she approached me.

"I suppose you've heard that we'll be staying on for a few days longer. Enrico is doing some business in town. Philippa and I are using this time to arrange for an interior designer to work on our new house."

"Bernie didn't tell me about your extended stay, but we're happy to have you here."

"Thank you. The older men are enjoying this area. They're even threatening to return from time to time to stay with Enrico and me."

"And how do you feel about that?" I teased.

She chuckled. "It's fine. They're fairly easy to have around, and I know both men have been lonely since their wives died."

"Is that why they've wanted to pressure the kids into marrying and living in Italy?" I asked.

Catarina shrugged. "That, and old age fears and promises. But they're sweet men who love their families."

We strolled together toward the hotel, and then I had to leave her to get to the office.

Rhonda was already there when I walked inside.

She looked up at me. "Have I got news for you! Harper and Luciano are in Ohio so he can meet her family. What do ya think of that?"

Relieved I wouldn't have to keep that news from her, I said, "I think it's sweet. A real old-fashioned gesture."

"You know preparing for dinner at my house, I mentioned something to Luciano about doing that," said Rhonda.

"You're going to take the credit for it?" I asked, chuckling.

"Why not? You know what an excellent matchmaker I am," said Rhonda. She broke down and laughed with me.

"I just spoke to Catarina," I said. "They're staying for a few more days in the guesthouse while Enrico does some business in town. She and Philippa will use this time to meet with an interior decorator for the new house."

"Nice. Any news on Chet and Philippa's romance?" Rhonda asked.

"I don't know because I didn't ask. But I have to tell you about seeing Brock on the beach. When he noticed me, he turned around and went in the opposite direction."

"About time that bastard learns we don't want anything to do with him," said Rhonda.

"We'll see. I think his ego won't allow him to keep away from us for long."

"I'm glad you're here because I have to leave for an hour or so to go see Evan in a school presentation this morning," said Rhonda. "He's being given some sort of prize in spelling."

"How nice," I said. "Take your time. I'm leaving later this afternoon to pick up Vaughn from the airport."

"It's fantastic that we can do things like this with our families," said Rhonda. "It's why I want to speak to you about a bonus for Bernie. Instead of giving him one at the end of the year, why don't we give him one now. Annette told me she and Bernie have been talking about taking a river cruise in Germany. This is an excellent time for them to go."

"Great idea. Once Thanksgiving is here, we'll be extra busy until Easter with no time off for any of us."

Rhonda stood. "Let's go tell him so he can plan the trip."

Later, after leaving Bernie's office, Rhonda turned to me. "Hiring Bernie as our General Manager was one of the best things we did."

"And Jean-Luc," I said. "Let's go see how he's doing with his new walking cast."

When we arrived in the kitchen, we found Jean-Luc directing his staff on meal preparations. Observing how he handled them with firm clarity, I was filled with satisfaction. Having seen Jonny Arno's behavior, I appreciated Jean-Luc's value and professional behavior.

"Where's Chet?" Rhonda asked him.

"He'll come in later today," said Jean-Luc.

"It's great to see you moving so well with your cast," I said.

He bobbed his head. "Better to be here than to be at home. I hadn't realized how active my boys are."

Rhonda and I exchanged glances but said nothing. Lindsay was a devoted mother.

On the way to pick up Vaughn from the airport, I thought about our office staff and how important they were, allowing Rhonda and me time off during the slower seasons.

When Vaughn headed out of the terminal with his overnight bag in hand, I couldn't help my excitement. He ignored the stares of people around him and kept his eyes focused on me as he made his way to my car.

"Hi, darling," he said in his deep musical voice as he opened the back door and tossed his luggage inside.

He climbed into the passenger seat, leaned over, and kissed me.

"Move along," said the policeman patrolling the area.

"More to come," said Vaughn buckling up. "I can't wait to get home and on the boat. It was a short trip, but a busy one. And I have a new contract with a company advertising yogurt."

I laughed. "Are we about to be inundated with yogurt?"

"I hope not. Not like last time with hot dogs." Once a certain company had learned that Vaughn liked their hot dogs, we'd been sent too many shipments of them.

"How are things at the hotel?" Vaughn asked. "You told me

about Brock's apology. No more problems? I don't like him constantly harassing you and Rhonda."

"We don't either. We'll see what he tries next. He keeps us on our toes."

Vaughn winked at me. "I like to keep you off your toes."

It was so good to have him home.

CHAPTER TWENTY-NINE

THE NEXT COUPLE OF DAYS PASSED WITH NO MAJOR problems at the hotel. At home, all was blissful. Robbie and Vaughn spent time on the boat and were even able to take the Ts and Liz on a short trip aboard it.

As many mornings as I could, I continued my walks on the beach. At the guesthouse where the Ferrara family had been staying, a new family had moved in. Life seemed to continue peacefully.

One afternoon, Rhonda and I were surprised when Enrico came into our office.

"Hello, Ann and Rhonda. I have some important news to tell you."

"Why don't you have a seat," I said, indicating a chair in front of my desk.

He sat down and took a deep breath. "I feel it's only right to let you know what's been going on because it will affect your hotel."

My heart fell. It sounded bad. I glanced at Rhonda and she, too, sensed bad news coming.

"Let's move to the conference table," I said, feeling the need to be business-like.

"Would you like water or anything else?" asked Rhonda as we stood.

"No, thank you," Enrico said, and followed us to the conference table in the corner of the office.

Once seated, Enrico faced us with a solemn expression. "I told you I invested in Osteria Arno. After the death of Jonny

Arno, the group decided to sell the restaurant." While we waited, he took another deep breath. "And my father, Angelo, and I, with the help of Giovanni, have decided to buy it."

"Wow! That's a surprise," said Rhonda, looking shocked.

"We bought it for a more than fair price and plan to make it an exceptional restaurant. We're working on building staff. That's where your hotel comes into play," said Enrico, giving us a worried look.

"Are you talking about using Chet at your restaurant?" I asked.

"Chet, Philippa, Harper, and Luciano. They're all working temporarily or part-time for you, right?"

Rhonda and I looked at one another and nodded.

"It's important for you to know that the four of them said they'd like to work for the new restaurant but wouldn't commit until I'd talked to you." Enrico studied us. "You have given them reason to be loyal, and I respect that."

"We had plans for all of them," I said. "But we wouldn't want to hold them back."

"They deserve to have bright futures," said Rhonda. "And if you can provide them with decent jobs and competitive pay, they should be allowed to go."

Enrico's shoulders sagged with relief. "You both are very generous, too generous. I truly appreciate that. We also want to give the young ones an opportunity to work hard and do well."

"What are you going to call this restaurant?" I asked.

A smile crossed Enrico's face. "Bella's. For my mother, Isabella. She and Giovanni's wife were best friends."

"What about the interior of the restaurant?" asked Rhonda. "That needs work."

"That is out of my hands. Catarina says it's awful but can easily be fixed." Enrico shrugged. "A price added to the cost of the sale."

"Well, it sounds as if it's going to be an improvement," I said. "I'm happy for you. Who is going to be your manager?"

"A man that used to work for Jonny and was fired by him. Someone Chet knows. A fine man," said Enrico. "Our four young people will each have a job of their own. They can tell you about it." He paused. "I have your permission to tell them you're okay with them doing this?"

"Yes," Rhonda and I said together.

Enrico stood with us. In the European way, he kissed each of us on one cheek, then the other. "*Grazie mille.*"

We walked him to the door and said goodbye.

"Well, that's a surprise," said Rhonda. "Just think. No more worries about fighting with another business in the area."

"And the kids deserve this chance," I added.

My cell phone rang, and I picked up the call.

"Ann? This is Chet. My friends and I are hoping to talk to you and Rhonda."

"Did Enrico call you?"

Chet laughed. "Just now. He told us we could discuss our plans with you."

"Come to the office. We'll wait for you here."

The call ended, and Rhonda and I opened the door to the four young people a few moments later.

We ushered them to the conference table and then listened as Chet began the conversation.

"We're grateful you're okay with our plans. I'll never forget how you took me in to work with Jean-Luc, and I appreciate your generosity in allowing me the opportunity to have my own restaurant. I've talked to several people from Osteria Arno who want to work with me."

"That's great news," I said. "And the rest of you?"

"I've talked to Liz and Angela about leaving the hotel.

They're going to implement some of the ideas I had," said Harper. "I'll be in charge of the bar at the new restaurant."

"And because I had no schedule, I was able to talk to Lauren and Lorraine about leaving," said Philippa. "At the new restaurant, I'll be handling hospitality and groups."

"And you, Luciano?" asked Rhonda.

"I'll be in charge of wine selections at the restaurant. Bolino wines will be featured and I'll be building a customer base in the U.S. My grandfather is excited about it."

"It couldn't work out better for all of you," I said.

Rhonda wagged a finger at them. "But please don't take any more of our staff with you."

"We won't," said Chet, raising his hand in a promise. "Enough of the original staff of Osteria Arno want to stay. Especially when they heard about the plans for the new restaurant."

"Bella's has a lovely ring to it," said Philippa. "Don't you think?"

"Yes, but more than that, we know we can have a pleasant relationship with you," I said.

"I've already thought of ways we can work together," said Harper. "We'll discuss it some other time." She rose. "Now, I have to go to work here."

"Me, too," said Chet, checking his watch.

They left, and Rhonda grinned at Luciano. "What was Ohio like?"

"Better than I thought. Harper's parents are really nice."

"I'm glad," Rhonda said. "You know, I'm very talented at putting people together."

I rolled my eyes, and Philippa laughed. "Not that again!"

Rhonda straightened with teasing indignation. "You'll see."

"I hope so," said Philippa. "Harper and Luciano make a great couple."

At home, I sat on the lanai with Vaughn sipping a glass of wine while he leaned back against a cushion on the couch facing me.

"I can't think of a better solution for Jonny's restaurant," I said. "Even the new name, Bella's, brings a sense of warmth to the place. I can't wait to see it when the decorating is done. Remember how awful it was?"

"As a matter of fact, I do," said Vaughn in his easygoing way. "I'm just happy you won't have to worry about any troubles from them." He pulled me close, and our conversation turned to other things.

For the next couple of weeks, things remained quiet but steady at the hotel. Jean-Luc didn't feel the need to hire a chef to replace Chet. Ricardo had done a great job as sous chef during Jean-Luc's absence and the rest of his staff had proven themselves to him by running the kitchen smoothly and efficiently under Ricardo's guidance.

I checked with Lorraine and Lauren. Though they were disappointed by the news, they were fine with Harper and Philippa not becoming a part of the team. Lauren had a friend who was interested.

Relieved there would be no hard feelings among our staff, Rhonda and I went about our business as two more weddings took place, along with the normal business meetings and luncheons.

Finally, when Rhonda could no longer stand it, Rhonda said to me. "C'mon. Let's go sneak a peek at Bella's. I can't wait to see what they're doing to it."

Rhonda pulled her convertible into the parking lot and stopped for a moment. "Looks a whole lot safer now."

I gazed at the vehicles owned by various workmen in the area. "No suspicious looking SUVs in sight."

She parked the car and we got out and stood to study the front of the building. Gone were the pink and gold touches. The double doors were now stained a rich mahogany brown.

We stepped inside and stayed in the entrance to gaze at the scene before us.

The gaudy pink patterned carpeting was replaced by a rich, deep green one. The walls were now a warm, soft sage. The crystal chandeliers remained in place and were an added touch.

"Wow! So much better," murmured Rhonda.

Philippa walked into the entrance and stopped. "What a surprise to see you here. What do you think?"

"It's lovely," I said. "Very welcoming."

"So much better," added Rhonda.

"We've done a lot of work outside with the landscaping. We've also added a beautiful patio. Come take a look," she said.

She led us to the side of the building where lush tropical plants and palm trees lined the edge of their property. In the middle of a tiled patio, a small fountain bubbled happily. Flowers and smaller tropical greenery edged the large patio. Tables with umbrellas covered some of the patio while comfortable seating arrangements were placed in the rest of the area.

"This makes all the sense in the world," I said. "It's sure to be a favorite spot for guests."

"We don't have the water as a background, but we can have a beautiful, restful garden," said Philippa.

"I love it," Rhonda said.

"How is everything coming along?" I asked.

Philippa clasped her hands. "Soon, we're going to have a private party for the crew, family, and friends. You and your husbands are invited, of course. I was just getting ready to send out invitations. Hold on, and I'll get yours."

While she was gone, Rhonda and I watched as a landscaper added an orange tree to the collection of plants.

"I'm really happy for them," said Rhonda. "I think it's going to be a success."

"Me, too. I'll be pleased to send guests their way."

Philippa joined us and handed each of us a creamy thick envelope. "It's not a restaurant opening party. It's a family thank-you celebration."

"I can't wait to help you and your family celebrate," I said.

She grinned at us. "We'll be serving lovely canapés."

"Of course," said Rhonda. "No place can match The Beach House Hotel without them."

We laughed together, and then Philippa was called away by a workman.

As we left the restaurant, Rhonda put her arm around me. "We did a good job in showing these kids how to do something right."

"I'd like to think so," I said. I knew it was a learning process. We were still discovering new things about true hospitality since we'd opened The Beach House Hotel.

CHAPTER THIRTY

SEVERAL DAYS LATER, VAUGHN AND I HEADED TO THE
private party at Bella's.

"Wait until you see the upgrades they've done to the place,"
I told him. "It's lovely."

"I'm more interested in those canapés you told me about,"
said Vaughn smiling.

"With Chet and his crew cooking, you know it's going to be
delicious. Jean-Luc helped Chet set up his kitchen. He's
become a mentor to him."

"Interesting. How does Philippa's family feel about Chet
now that he's part of the family business?"

"I'm curious to find out," I said. "I've purposely avoided
discussing it with Rhonda."

Vaughn laughed. "Wise choice."

We parked in front of the restaurant and went up to the
front door. Beside it stood two tall pots holding a variety of
colorful flowers.

Inside, we walked to a small reception desk.

From behind it, Philippa beamed at us. "Welcome to
Bella's. We hope you have an enjoyable time." Then, coming
around it, she hugged me. "I'm so glad you're here. I can't wait
for you to be part of this celebration."

She and Vaughn exchanged quick hugs and then we moved
on to allow guests behind us to enter. Standing in the
entrance, Vaughn gazed around him. "Wow! This is a lot
different."

"Follow me. I can't wait for you to see the patio. It's

stunning."

We walked outside and saw Catarina and Enrico standing beside a table where the two grandfathers were seated.

"*Buonasera*," said Enrico, approaching me and kissing me on both cheeks before shaking hands with Vaughn.

Catarina and I hugged a greeting and then I turned to Angelo and Giovanni.

"This is such an exciting evening. Everything looks beautiful." I indicated the patio with a sweep of my arm. "And I love this spot. So special."

"My Bella would be very honored," said Angelo, his eyes filling.

"My wife would be happy, too," Giovanni said. "Our families are so close."

Rhonda and Will joined us, and I crept away, eager to see the kitchen.

On my way there, I was pleasantly surprised to see so many employees of our hotel as guests in attendance. It reminded me that Osteria Arno was doomed to fail from the beginning because it had no cohesive staff. With Jonny in charge, it couldn't.

I peeked into the kitchen. Because no meals were being served, it was less hectic than it might've been, but the small crew was working together to prepare trays of food, including the promised canapés, including my favorite made with smoked salmon and caviar.

Chet saw me and walked over. "How does it look?"

"Very organized and very professional," I said, smiling at him.

"I didn't realize when you and Rhonda hired me, my whole life would change," he said. "Thanks."

"We're both very proud of you," I said, as Rhonda joined me.

"You're doing a great job," she said. "C'mon, Annie. Catarina says we must join her on the patio for a toast."

"I'll follow you," said Chet.

On the patio, Enrico stood near the fountain, holding a glass high.

"Thank you, friends and family, for joining us tonight in a celebration of not only this restaurant but of bringing new people into the family. They are creating something beautiful in loving memory of two *bellissima* ladies—Isabella Ferrara and Lucia Bolino. It was their wish that their two grandchildren marry, but Philippa and Luciano have chosen well for themselves."

I joined everyone in clapping, feeling my eyes sting with unexpected tears.

"Now," he continued, "we have other women in the family to honor. My beautiful wife, Catarina, my daughter, Philippa, and Harper Lewis, who is here with her parents." He gave a little bow. "We welcome you."

"Yes, it's such a pleasure," said Catarina coming to stand beside Enrico.

Chet stepped up and stood facing the gathering in his black-checked pants and white chef's jacket. "This isn't exactly how I planned it, but it seems the perfect time." He knelt in front of Philippa. "I've loved you from those many months ago in New York. My time with you here has only deepened those feelings. I can't imagine a day without you by my side, cheering me on. I promise to show you the depth of my love every day. Philippa Ferrara, will you marry me?"

Philippa beamed at him. "Yes, oh yes. I love you, Chet!"

Chet rose and pulled her into his arms.

While they clung together, I dabbed at my eyes with a tissue Rhonda handed me. I wasn't the only one touched by his proposal. Catarina, Enrico, and the two older gentlemen had tears glistening on their cheeks.

"Bravo," cried Enrico. "You did a superb job, Chet."

Philippa looked at her father with surprise. "You knew about this?"

Enrico proudly nodded. "Of course. I am your father."

Catarina and I exchanged understanding glances.

"This is the best party ever," said Rhonda, wiping her eyes. "I'm going to be a mess when the time comes for my Willow to marry."

I gave her a quick hug. She was a tender mess at every wedding. It was one of her endearing qualities.

A few months later, Rhonda and I sat with others waiting for Philippa and her father to walk into the library at The Beach House Hotel. The backs of the chairs formed into a circle were covered with white cloth and festooned with orange bougainvillea and deep orange ribbons.

At the front of the room, a dais for the minister held a white bible and a small arrangement of orange and white flowers, including orchids. It was flanked by large, round white candles.

Catarina was sitting with the two grandfathers closest to the altar. Several staff members of both Bella's and The Beach House Hotel filled chairs beyond her.

Dressed in gray slacks and a white shirt, Chet stood at the front of the room with Luc as his best man. On the other side of the dais, Harper waited in a deep russet tea-length dress that suited the strawberry-blond color of her hair.

The guitar music began, and the doors to the room opened.

Time seemed to stand still as Enrico entered with Philippa on his arm.

Rhonda was already in tears as Philippa, looking like an

angel in a long white silk dress, entered the room and gazed at her bridegroom with a sweet smile.

Beside me, Vaughn squeezed my hand to show me he understood my own tears.

The love story between these two young people was something Rhonda and I took to heart. It was, in a way, part of our ongoing journey. There would be many more weddings at The Beach House Hotel. But we saw each one as an opportunity to provide families with a lovely setting for such a ceremony. A setting we'd worked hard for.

"Pretty special, huh?" Rhonda whispered.

"Oh, yes," I murmured.

Later, at the reception that followed the wedding ceremony, I gazed around at the group of family and friends. Chet and Philippa represented so much of what Rhonda and I had wanted when we created the hotel. We'd hoped The Beach House Hotel would become a peaceful, elegant place where people could relax and be themselves. Where they could celebrate life's special moments. We didn't realize how each guest would make the hotel an even better place because of who they were.

"And to think this wedding started with canapés. Who woulda thunk it," said Rhonda taking one from a tray offered to her and popping it in her mouth.

I felt my smile. I could never have a better partner. We'd surprised a lot of people with our success and would continue to do so with love and laughter.

Thank you for reading *Canapes at The Beach House Hotel*. If you enjoyed this book, please help other readers discover it by leaving a review on your favorite site. It's such a nice thing to do.

For your further enjoyment, the other books in The Beach House Hotel Series are available on all sites. Here are the Universal links:

Breakfast at The Beach House Hotel:
https://books2read.com/u/bpkoq4

Lunch at The Beach House Hotel:
https://books2read.com/u/3GWvp3

Dinner at The Beach House Hotel:
https://books2read.com/u/4N1yDW

Christmas at The Beach House Hotel:
https://books2read.com/u/38gZvd

Margaritas at The Beach House Hotel:
https://books2read.com/u/bMRrP7

Dessert at The Beach House Hotel:
https://books2read.com/u/mV6kX6

Coffee at The Beach House Hotel:
https://books2read.com/u/bOnE7A

High Tea at The Beach House Hotel:
https://books2read.com/u/mgN9AK

Nightcaps at The Beach House Hotel:
https://books2read.com/u/mBA2oy

Bubbles at The Beach House Hotel:
https://books2read.com/u/meGgRV

Sign up for my newsletter and get a free story. I keep my newsletters short and fun with giveaways, recipes, and the latest must-have news about me and my books. Welcome! Here's the link:
https://BookHip.com/RRGJKGN

ABOUT THE AUTHOR

A *USA Today* **Best-Selling Author**, Judith Keim is a hybrid author who both has a publisher and self-publishes. Ms. Keim writes heart-warming novels about women who face unexpected challenges, meet them with strength, and find love and happiness. Her best-selling books are based, in part, on many of the places she's lived or visited and on the interesting people she's met, creating believable characters and realistic settings her many loyal readers love. Ms. Keim loves to hear from her readers and appreciates their enthusiasm for her stories.

Ms. Keim enjoyed her childhood and young-adult years in Elmira, New York, and now makes her home in Boise, Idaho, with her husband and their lovable miniature Dachshunds, Wally and Kacy, and other members of her family.

While growing up, she was drawn to the idea of writing stories from a young age. Books were always present, being read, ready to go back to the library, or about to be discovered. All in her family shared information from the books in general conversation, giving them a wealth of knowledge and vivid imaginations.

"I hope you've enjoyed this book. If you have, please help other readers discover it by leaving a review on the site of your choice. And please check out my other books and series:"

The Hartwell Women Series
The Beach House Hotel Series
Fat Fridays Group
The Salty Key Inn Series
The Chandler Hill Inn Series
Seashell Cottage Books
The Desert Sage Inn Series
Soul Sisters at Cedar Mountain Lodge
The Sanderling Cove Inn Series
The Lilac Lake Inn Series
The Lilac Lake Books

"ALL THE BOOKS ARE NOW AVAILABLE IN AUDIO on iTunes! So fun to have these characters come alive!"

Ms. Keim can be reached at **www.judithkeim.com**

And to like her author page on Facebook and keep up with the news, go to: **http://bit.ly/2pZWDgA**

To receive notices about new books, follow her on Book Bub:

https://www.bookbub.com/authors/judith-keim

And here's a link to where you can sign up for her periodic newsletter! **http://bit.ly/2OQsb7s**

She is also on Twitter @judithkeim, LinkedIn, and Goodreads. Come say hello!

ACKNOWLEDGMENTS

As always, I am eternally grateful to my team of editors, Peter Keim and Lynn Mapp, my book cover designer, Lou Harper, and my narrator for Audible and iTunes, Angela Dawe. They are the people who take what I've written and help turn it into the book I proudly present to you, my readers! I also wish to thank my coffee group of writers who listen and encourage me to keep on going. Thank you, Peggy Staggs, Lynn Mapp, Cate Cobb, Nikki Jean Triska, Joanne Pence, Melanie Olsen, and Megan Bryce. And to you, my fabulous readers, I thank you for your continued support and encouragement. Without you, this book would not exist. You are the wind beneath my wings.